The Little Acrobat

By Kate Greaves

Illustrations by Isobelle Greaves

DEDICATION

This book is dedicated to my grandparents, Florence and Sam Copeman, and my mother, Mollie Palmer, all of whom were the inspiration for this story.

And the book is written for Isobelle, Livia, William and Arto, four of Florence and Sam's precious great-great grandchildren.

CONTENTS

ACKNOWLEDGMENTS

I would like to thank all those who have given me the encouragement to write this book. My family and friends who gave such valuable feedback. Rebecca Smith and Carole Burns from the University of Southampton who believed in the project. And my grand-daughter, Isobelle Greaves, who patiently drew the illustrations – just like Millie might have.

Prologue

The little acrobat waits in the old nursery cupboard.

The children have long gone. No one has been here for years, but he's learnt to be patient.

He's tucked away high on a shelf, wrapped in crinkly tissue paper, in a box with the other circus figures.

Not long to wait now............

Act 1

March 1915
Everything is Different Now...

'Race you home,' Mary says as the school bell rings.

Millie looks back at the long schoolroom. Has she forgotten something? Miss Simpson is cleaning the chalk off the blackboard. The battered wooden desks are clear, the chairs turned upside down on top of them.

'No. You go on,' Millie says. She doesn't want to run, there's stuff to think about. There's the war to think about. Everything's so different now. She puts on her coat and rams her hat on her head. She bangs the school door open.

'What's up?' Mary asks. She's waiting outside.

Millie shuffles her feet as she walks. Miss Simpson had told them they had to be careful what they said about the war when they were out in public. About where their fathers are in France or what they're doing in the army, or the navy. Because someone might be listening and then important, secret information could get back to the enemy. Has she said anything about Papa? Nothing's easy anymore. 'Spies,' she says.

'What about them?'

'Do you think there are any round here?'

'No idea!'

'Well, that's what I mean. How would you know? They're not going to go around with a big notice round their neck with *SPY* on it, are they?'

'They might,' Mary laughs, skipping in front of Millie. She's lifting up the hems of her coat and skirt as she dances over the puddles on the path. Her wooden clogs click as she walks and clatter as she runs. 'And on their hat too.'

'Is your spy a man or a lady?'

'Man, I should think.'

'Why?'

Mary stops dancing. 'Man, definitely. Me Mam wouldn't have time to be a spy. She says it's only men as have time to loiter about getting under everyone's feet. Well, that's what she said about me Dad before he went into the army.'

Millie laughs. Mumma said that about Papa too before he went away. She says, 'I bet we'd make jolly good spies if we tried.'

'Oh, we'd be the best,' Mary says. 'We're a right pair of nosey parkers!'

Millie remembers she's going to the music hall tonight. 'See you on Monday,' she calls and heads for home.

'Can I do some drawing?' Millie asks.

'Yes, but don't be too long, tea's nearly ready.'

Millie takes the grey tile and a piece of chalk from the kitchen table drawer. As she draws, the chalk scrapes on the slate.

'I wish I could have a proper drawing book.'

'Yes, well,' Mumma says. 'If wishes were horses, beggars would ride.'

'You always say that. And I still don't know what it means. I don't want a horse, I want a drawing book. Not just this scratchy slate.'

'I'll ask Ted to look out some of the old theatre posters for you. We could cut them up and use the backs to draw on. I'm sure I can find you a pencil.'

Mumma's only trying to help, and having the thick poster paper and a pencil is better than any slate. But Millie longs for a drawing book.

'What you doing, Millie?' Daisy asks.

'I'm drawing the tram that will take Mumma and me to the theatre tonight.'

'Me see.' Millie makes some room for her little sister on the bench.

'No touching,' she says. 'You only smudge the chalk.'

Mumma says, 'Yes, and then you get it everywhere. So no touching, Miss Daisy.'

'Finished,' Millie says, and Mumma comes to have a look.

'Oh, that's so good, Millie. And look there are two people sitting on the tram, I wonder who they can be?'

'You and me,' Millie says.

Mumma laughs. 'Of course. Are we going to the theatre or coming home?'

'Going.'

'Well, we'd better have our tea, or the tram will go without us.'

At the Theatre

Millie feels like a princess. The huge wicker props basket is her special place, and, this week, Ted, the Stage Hand, has found her a big purple cushion to sit on.

'For your throne, your majesty,' he'd said. She'd thanked him just like a queen might, called him 'Sir Ted'.

The basket is so big that, even though she's now nine years old, her feet still don't touch the floor. She looks at her battered, black button boots. She hates them, longs to grow out of them. Wishes she could wear clogs like Mary. No more bruising and pinching from the button hook. They're hand-me-downs like the rest of her clothes. Will she ever get anything new?

From where she sits, Millie can see the stage of the great gold and red theatre. It's her special Friday treat for helping Mumma at home, with the washing, doing shopping and looking after Daisy. Usually she'd be asleep in bed beside Daisy, watched over by their neighbour, Martha, the lady who lives on the other side of the landing from them. But Friday's are her night.

Here, in the wings, is excitement, bustle and noise. Pretty ladies come by and give her a hug as they run onto the stage to dance behind Mumma. Sometimes they wear tights and short frilly skirts, and as they run on stage the audience whistles and shouts.

Acrobats and jugglers practise in the wings and Millie laughs when they pull funny faces at her. One man can wrap himself into a knot. He's a con-tor-tion-ist, has double joints. She's so fascinated mimicking the shapes he can make, she nearly falls off the basket.

The man in charge, Mr Albert, is very stern and shouts at the performers, but he always smiles at Millie and says she's the miniature of her mother. He's told her that she'll be a star one day and she knows it's the thing she wants most in the world. To be a music hall star, just like Mumma.

Millie can feel the heat from the big lamps that light the stage. Sometimes they blow out with a loud pop and Ted has to come and relight them before the next act. Why do people throw things on the stage and try to hit him? He's such a nice, smiley man. And her friend.

Mumma's on stage, performing one of those songs that everyone sings now. Millie knows all the songs and sings along with them quietly. This one is like a march and all about men going to the war and how everyone at home will miss them when they go, and kiss them when they come home again.

Mumma's wearing a long dress of red, white and blue. Her dark hair is piled high and she wears a straw hat with a red, white and blue ribbon. And she walks around the stage like a queen. She uses her flouncy Union Jack umbrella to point at people in the audience.

Tonight, behind the curtain at the back of the stage, two soldiers are sitting at a desk arranging some forms and piles of silver coins. One of them stands and straightens his thick khaki jacket, takes off his hat and puts it back on his head. Is he going to stand to attention? He's only just sat down, when Ted raises the curtain so the audience can see them.

Mumma and most of the girls leave the stage and walk down steps into the audience, still singing, the band still playing. Men are starting to walk onto the stage and up to the desk. Millie sees Joe, Martha's son. He's one of the first on the stage. As he turns from the table he has a great smile on his face and, catching sight of Millie, does a funny wave with his hand.

'Look out there, Millie,' Ted says. At first, as she peeks from behind the heavy curtain, Millie can see only the foggy haze of cigarette and cigar smoke, but then she catches sight of Mumma walking up and down the aisles of the great theatre. She's stepping in time to the music and still singing, but as she passes men she touches them on the shoulder, and they stand and walk towards the stage. Some of the dancers have moved up into the higher seating in the circle, and are showing the men sitting up there how to get to the stage too. Soon there are two queues of men in front of the desk and Mumma and the dancers return to the stage and sing more marching songs as the men behind them give their name, receive a coin, and are told where to report the next day.

Papa had joined the army ages ago. She and Daisy had held his hand as he marched out through the town behind the military band, until Mumma caught them up and held them back. They had waved and waved. He'd looked so smart in his uniform and happy. Was he happy to be leaving them?

'He's good at running away, your Papa,' Mumma said as they'd watched.

'Why's he running away?'

'This time he says he must fight in the war.'

Millie wanted to ask about the other times he'd run away, but looking at Mumma, she changed her mind. She just held Mumma's hand instead.

It isn't the same without him. Mumma's taken in ironing, 'to help make ends meet' and Millie's been given the task of nursemaid to Daisy.

She sees Mr Albert at the other side of the stage. He's watching the soldiers, counting on his fingers as each one moves from the table. He'll lose his place if anyone talks to him. But then she sees he's got a little black notebook and is writing things in it.

Ted joins her at the end of the show and they watch everyone take their final bow and sing God Save the King. This is Millie's chance to sing and she sings out. "Ere, you're in fine form tonight, Millie,' Ted says. 'Just like your Mumma. She's a wonderful woman. The recruiting sergeants are talking about giving her a special medal. Over 300 men signed up tonight.'

'Where are the men going, Ted?' Millie asks.

'Off to the army. They'll be in France soon.'

'Are you going?'

'No. It's me chest, Millie. I got asthma. I tried to join, but they wouldn't 'ave me.'

'What's asthma?'

'It stops me breathing. I lose me breath.'

Millie looks at the bustle of activity on the stage.

'I wish Papa had asthma.'

'Funny, that's just what your Mumma said when I told her they'd turned me down. Now come along, young lady, let's get you back to the dressing rooms, she'll be ready to take you home.'

They weave their way down the stairs at the back of the stage and along the narrow dimly lit corridor, past Mr Albert's office, past the stairs down to the toilet, until they reach a room with a green door with silver stars on it.

'Flo, you decent yet?' Ted calls.

'Yes, of course I am, you silly old fool, come on in.' Mumma is sitting in front of the huge mirror and smiles at them when they open the door. 'Did you enjoy the show, Millie?'

'It was wonderful. But I liked the con-tor-tion-ist best I think.'

'Oh I see. Well, that's really put me in my place. After all my hard work recruiting soldiers and you're impressed by Bendy Barry.' When she's saying funny things, Mumma speaks with her Irish accent, lilting, singalong. Millie uses it herself sometimes. Papa says that she's a good mimic, has a good ear.

Ted says, 'Better go now, or old Albert'll have my guts for garters. Bye Millie, see you soon.'

'Bye, Ted. Thank you.'

Millie walks over to Mumma and looks in the mirror at their reflections. 'I did love the show this evening, Mumma. When you were out with the audience, the sergeants were tapping their feet under the table, and one was almost dancing. He was like a puppet.'

'Did you see Joe?'

'Yes, he was one of the first on stage.'

'He's only just 17. What do they want taking him at that age? How will I face Martha?'

'Isn't it good to go to war?'

'It's good for the country that men join up, Millie. But it's awful for the people they leave behind. We know that, don't we?'

Millie nods. When Papa went away, she had a pain in her heart, right in her centre. 'Poor Martha,' she says.

Mumma gives her a hug. 'Let's go home and see that funny little sister of yours'. As they get to the door, Mumma says, 'Silly me! I nearly forgot. Ted found these for you.' It's a roll of old theatre posters, tied up with string. Millie sighs.

'Cheer up. I know it's not a book, but at least you can keep the pictures you draw now.'

Outside, the city streets are shining after heavy rain and they run to catch their tram back to the room in the tenement block where they live.

Shopping

'You done any spying yet?' Mary says. She's carrying an empty cotton shopping bag in one hand and a piece of paper in the other.

'Well, I spy you're going shopping,' Millie says.

'That's not what I meant,' Mary says, aiming her shopping bag at Millie's arm. 'Real spying.'

The girls walk along the pavement together towards the market. It's busy. Families are out and about getting food for the weekend. Some of the men are in uniform.

'I heard Mumma talking to Joe this morning. He has to tell Martha about him joining the army.'

'What did he say?'

'Well, he reckoned that if he just told his Mam he was in support, she wouldn't worry.'

'And is he in support?'

'Course not. Mumma said he has to tell Martha the truth before some busybody does.'

'There'll be a row.'

'Yes, he's only 17. They took his name last night, 'cos he told them he was 18, and they gave him the King's shilling.'

The market square is on the other side of the road and the girls take care to wait for the horses and carts, the trams, and one or two cars to pass.

'Now,' Mary shouts, and they dash across.

They head for the greengrocers' stall. There are potatoes, cabbages, carrots, parsnips, swedes, onions and a few cooking apples for sale. Millie looks at her list. When it's her turn she tells the boy, 'Can I have some carrots and potatoes, please?'

'Pound of each?'

'Yes, please. And a cabbage too.'

The greengrocer says, 'You make sure you give young Millie the best, Harry.'

The boy raises his eyes to heaven. 'I know, Dad,' he says. Millie smiles. They know whose daughter she is. They'd be in trouble from Mumma if they dared to give her a wilted cabbage, or a rotten potato.

Millie hands over her shopping bag and Harry puts the vegetables in and hands it back to her.

'Six pence to you, Mill,' he says. She takes the money from the blue velvet purse that hangs around her neck, and hands it over. Then she waits whilst Mary buys vegetables and apples.

'What about you?' Millie asks. 'What spying have you done?'

'Well, I heard Auntie Annie tell me Mam that she's going to work in the arm-a-ments factory.'

'Did she? That's men's work.'

'That's what me Mam said, but Auntie Annie said, 'There aren't any men left and they need fit lasses, so I joined.''

'Will they pay her?'

'Yes, and give her a good meal. Me Mam was pleased about that. 'You're just skin and bone, our Annie,' she said.'

The girls are walking more slowly now, carrying the heavy bags. 'Can you come out this afternoon?' Millie asks.

'Not sure. Why?'

'I've promised Mumma I'd take Daisy out to the park. The soldiers who joined up yesterday will be there practising their marching. They won't be very good at it. You're not supposed to laugh, but it's quite funny.'

'I'll ask. Good spying, by the way.'

'Yes, and you.'

The bag is much heavier now, but she's nearly home. Fancy having to work in a factory, with arm-a-ments. That's hard work. Bert, the man who lives above them, works at the factory. But he's on nights, so he sleeps during the day. He's a night watchman. His wife Gladys is very jolly. But he's grumpy, and shouts or bangs on the ceiling of their room if Millie or Daisy are being noisy when he's trying to sleep.

She's walking up the wide concrete stairway that leads to their landing, when she realises she hasn't told Mary about Mr Albert, at the theatre, counting the soldiers and making notes in his book. Bother.

.

Mary Comes to Tea

Millie doesn't see Mary again until they walk to school together on Monday. 'You should come and see our beds,' Millie tells her. 'They're brilliant.'

'Why?'

'Don't you want to come?'

'No, why are they brilliant?'

'Oh, 'cos they're in a cupboard. You wouldn't even know they were there when the doors are shut.'

'I have a little bed, but when I was a baby me Mam put me in the bottom of a chest of drawers.'

"Come and have tea and then you can see. Will your Mam let you?'

'I'll ask.'

'Good. I've got something important to show you.'

'Don't be shy, Mary,' Mumma says when Millie brings her home a few days later. 'It's lovely to see you. I've baked a sultana cake.'

'Come on,' Millie says. 'We'd better wash our hands.'

Millie takes Mary out onto the landing again. In the corner is the huge white sink.

'Use this,' Millie says handing Mary the large block of green soap. 'If you work up a lather, you can make big bubbles, and blow them away into the air.'

Daisy comes out to see them and tries to catch the bubbles. They are soon laughing.

'Shh,' Mumma says, from the doorway. 'You'll wake Bert and then there'll be trouble. Come and have your tea now.'

The girls dry their hands on the striped towel hanging from the hook beside the sink. Mary looks around. 'Is that where Martha lives?'

'Yes, and Joe. And Grandad. He's always running away, and they have to get the police to help find him.'

'What's in this cupboard?' Mary asks.

'Oh, that's the toilet. We share it with Martha. There's one on every floor, but ours is the cleanest.'

'You're lucky. Ours is in the yard outside.'

Millie shivers. 'When we were on tour a few years ago, we stayed at a place that had one at the bottom of the garden. Mumma was so cross with Papa that we nearly came home. He had to find us somewhere else to stay very quickly.'

'Sorry for making too much noise, Mrs Elliot,' Mary says as they climb up to the table.

'Thank you, Mary,' Mumma says. 'But, you weren't to know about Bert. And it's lovely for Millie to have a friend to tea.'

The cake is full of sultanas, and Mumma lets them both have a second piece. Mary says thank you lots of times and cuts her slices into little pieces. She eats them very slowly, with her eyes closed, but smiling. And then she makes sure that she eats every crumb left on her plate.

Mumma says, 'Mary, I have a good piece of this cake left over. Would your mother mind if I wrap it up and you take it home, do you think?'

'Oh, Mrs Elliot. She won't mind at all. Thank you very much.'

'Can I show Mary my bed cupboard, Mumma?'

'Yes, but take your shoes off first, I've only just changed the linen.'

Whilst Mumma is busy doing the washing-up in the big white sink on the landing, Millie takes a letter from the mantelpiece. Then she opens the cupboard doors and shows Mary her bed. It's a mattress on a shelf.

'That's brilliant,' Mary says. And they take off their shoes and climb in. Daisy joins them.

'My bed too,' she says.

'You can shut the doors as well and turn on the gas mantle,' Millie explains.

'Where do your parents sleep?'

'In the cupboard next door.

'I'd love a bed like this.'

'You said you had a bed of your own. You don't have to share.'

'Yes, but it's very small and the mattress is really old and lumpy. And it can get really cold. This is snug.'

'I want to show you something.' It's a letter from Papa.

March 1915

From ▬▬▬▬ *Camp*

> *My dearest darling girls,*
>
> *How are you all? I have been missing you so much, but I hear from good sources that you're doing sterling work for the war effort. I wish I was there to help you.*
>
> *Life is busy here. I can't tell you much about what I'm doing, but I'm very lucky and I'm working with horses again. My job is to train them for their big adventure. I like working with these beautiful animals, reminds me of my days in the circus before we were a family.*

> *I will be working here for a little while yet, so I may see you soon.*
>
> *Millie and Daisy be good for Mumma. Flo, I know you're cross with me, but this is vital work and I'm quite safe. You should be getting the money through by now, so hopefully life is a little more comfortable for you.*
>
> *Your ever loving,*
>
> *Frank*

'See the big black lines. They're where Papa wrote something he shouldn't have, like where he was, or where he was going, or the work he was doing.'

'Secret information,' Mary said.

'Yes, and Mumma said that the officer in charge would have crossed out the secrets to be on the safe side.'

'So spies couldn't get it.'

'Yes.'

Mumma walks back with the clean pots and starts to put them away.

'It's a lovely letter, Millie. You're Dad really loves you, doesn't he?'

'Don't you get letters from your Dad?' Millie asks.

'No. But then me Mam says he's not one with words. He can't write.'

Millie doesn't know what to say. Mary is looking as if she might cry. Mumma opens the cupboard doors wide and says, 'Mary, we need to get you home, my love. Come on Daisy, Millie, get your shoes on and we'll all walk Mary home.'

'There's no need, Mrs Elliot.'

'There's every need and it's our pleasure.' And Mumma sings them all the way back to Mary's house.

'See you tomorrow, Millie. Thank you for tea, Mrs Elliot. And for the cake.'

'Our pleasure,' Mumma says. 'Come and see us again soon, Mary.'

As the three of them walk home, Mumma says, 'You know, Millie, not everyone is as lucky as we are. You're old enough to understand that now. Think of other people a bit more.'

'We don't have very much.'

'No, we don't. But we have a lot more than many other

people.'

'I don't know what I would do if Papa couldn't write to us.'

'Well, Papa is in England, so he has time to write now. When he goes to France, likes Mary's father, he might not be able to write then. He might not have the time.'

'I don't like war,' Millie says. 'Everything is different.'

'Yes, and we just have to make the best of it.'

A few minutes later they arrive home. Mumma says, 'How about a nice cup of warm milk before bed?'

At the Park with Daisy

Millie and Daisy are at the park and Daisy is dancing around in her funny way, mostly hopping and wiggling her bottom, waving her arms in the air. They're giving a concert to their dolls that are propped against a large tree. Millie is the announcer, the com-pere, and singing the tune, *Daisy, Daisy, give me your answer do...* She hadn't really wanted to come, but she'd promised Daisy that if she ate all her bread and dripping she'd bring her, and Papa says you should always keep your promises. She's just wondering if he keeps all of his, when the song ends. She walks towards Daisy clapping her hands together and smiling at their little audience.

'Ladies and gentlemen, please put your hands together for Little Daisy Elliot, the most beautiful dancer in the whole world.'

'More dancing,' says Daisy. Daisy loves to dance, so Millie gives in and lets her do two more dances. First she sings *Pop Goes the Weasel,* but for the last dance Millie insists she sings a proper song as Daisy dances.

'Ladies and gentlemen, now the most wonderful Misses Elliot will perform for you, *It's a Long Way to Tipperary.*'

Millie takes her place at the front of the imaginary stage, stands up straight and starts to sing. She marches around with her head held high, but always making sure she's facing the front. Just as Mumma does on the stage. When you're singing you mustn't turn your back on an audience, because your voice goes to the back of the stage and then they can't hear you. It's all about a young Irish lad coming to London and being very excited to find a city full of riches and fun.

She's just going to sing the chorus when she sees Mr Albert. He's standing not far from them across the park and he's talking to a thin man who has a brown bowler hat and a brown striped suit. They look odd. Shifty. As if what they're doing isn't right, but Millie isn't sure why.

Something tells her that she should keep singing and she sings loudly, marching backwards and forwards on the grass. Daisy is bobbing around her, flapping her arms like a bird. Whilst she sings, Millie watches as Mr Albert takes out his notebook, tears out some pages and gives them to the other man. And the man in the hat takes his wallet and gives Mr Albert some paper money, lots of it. They talk with their heads together and then looking over their shoulders to see if anyone is watching. Why haven't they seen us?

Millie sings the chorus. She knows it so well she hardly has to think about the words. The young man is remembering his love in Ireland and that's where he's left his heart.

There's the sound of clapping and Ted joins them. Millie'd been so busy watching Mr Albert and his friend that she hadn't noticed Ted.

'I could hear you right past that tree. Bravo, well done,' he calls and starts to whistle, his fingers in his mouth.

'Ted,' says Millie. 'Did you see Mr Albert just now?'

'No, was 'e here auditioning you?' Ted laughs at his joke.

Millie's serious. 'No, he was over by that tree talking to a funny looking man in a bowler hat, and the funny man gave him lots of money for pages from his notebook.'

'Millie, I didn't see them. Perhaps you were imagining it. You've a mighty 'magination.'

Adults are always doing this. She tells them important things and they say she's imagining it.

Daisy's stopped dancing and has gone over to sit with the dolls. The spell's broken, the concert finished.

'I think she's tired,' Millie says. 'I'd better get home.'

'Shall I walk back with you?' Ted asks.

'No, we'll go straight home. Thanks anyway.' Millie's cross with him. If he won't take her seriously, why should she be his friend?

'See you soon, then,' he says. 'We'll see you Friday, anyway.'

'Perhaps,' Millie says. 'I might have to look after Daisy on Friday. Come on, Daise. You take your doll and I'll carry mine. Bye, Ted.'

Ted looks sad. Serves him right, he should've listened to me.

As they walk home she thinks about what she's seen. Maybe she could ask Mr Albert when she sees him again, but she's not sure, there was something about the way the two men had been talking that makes her think that asking questions wouldn't be safe.

After tea, Millie tries to draw a picture of Mr Albert and his friend on one of the pages cut from the theatre posters. Mumma has found her a small stub of a pencil, sharpened to a point with the vegetable knife.

'What you drawing?' Daisy asks.

'Go away,' Millie says. 'I don't want you here.'

Daisy starts to cry and Mumma comes in from the landing looking cross. 'For goodness sake, whatever's the matter now?'

Millie gives up. It just looks like two men standing in a wood. It could be anyone. She screws it up and throws it on the fire. Bother.

Papa

Mumma's busy. She's been tidying and polishing, washing and ironing, blacking the range, making the girls put their toys away. And she isn't singing like she usually does when she's happy. Papa's coming home. Not for good, he'll have to go back to the army again, but he's coming home to see them and Millie thinks it might be one of the best days of her life.

'Isn't it good that Papa's coming home?' she asks.

'Don't ask such damn silly questions, child. Of course it's good. Why wouldn't it be?'

'Will you be pleased to see him?' Millie persists. 'I can't wait.'

'If I can get this place looking reasonable before he arrives I'll be pleased to see him. He'll be gone again before we know it and I don't want to be fussing with cleaning and washing whilst he's here.

Later Mumma says, 'Be a good girl and take Daisy to Martha's.'

Martha seems excited too. 'It'll be lovely to see your Papa again, he's a real gent.'

Daisy starts to cry. 'Me go too,' she shouts.

'No lass, you stay with me. We're going to make some buns for tea. You can take one home for your Papa when he arrives.'

Millie knows it's best to just go. 'Bye, Daisy,' she calls, as she shuts the door.

When she gets back, Mumma is looking in the mirror examining her face. Millie sees that her hair is piled high on her head and she has her large brimmed blue felt hat ready to put on. It's sunny outside so no coats today.

'Get changed quickly now, Millie. We don't want to be late.'

Millie puts on her dress. It's made of blue cotton, has a square collar trimmed in white, and long sleeves. To keep it clean, she puts a clean white pinafore over the top. She rams her straw hat on her head, finds her cotton gloves and puts them on too.

Mumma stops as they get to the door and looks back at the room. 'Well, it mightn't be very special, but it's as clean as a new pin. Those flowers you got from the market this morning look very pretty.'

The flowers are sitting in a glass jar in the middle of table and Millie thinks again how much she likes living here. It's one of the few places she's lived that really feels like home.

'Can we stay here forever?' she asks.

'We'll see,' says Mumma. 'Quick, we mustn't miss the tram.'

Millie has never seen anything like it. She doesn't know whether to look or not. After a minute or two, curiosity gets the better of her and she looks around.

She can see rows of ambulances parked at the front of the station. Some of the ambulances are horse drawn, others have engines. Stretchers are being loaded into the back of each ambulance and on the stretchers are men with red stained bandages on their heads, legs, arms, tummies. Everyone is dressed like soldiers, except for a few nurses with their light grey dresses, white aprons, and hats that cover their hair.

Mumma says, 'Don't wander off, child. I wasn't expecting this.'

As they walk into the station, Millie can see the high glass ceiling and the steam from the trains. The noise of the shunting and hiss of the trains is deafening. There are so many people and they all seem to be shouting. She clings onto Mumma's hand and skirt.

There are stretchers everywhere in the station. They're lined up along the platforms, so close together that the nurses are finding it difficult to walk between them. There are stretchers under the notice boards and around the ticket office. And on every stretcher is a different man, some still in uniform and wearing white bandages with red stains, like someone has been around with a pot of dark red paint.

There are people like them there too. Normal people in ordinary clothes. Mumma looks at the notice board to see when Papa's train is arriving.

Millie remembers that Papa's brother, Jack, is in France now and wonders if he's been hurt like all these men. Is he here too?

Looking for him, she sees the thin man with the brown bowler hat. He's still wearing his brown stripy suit. He's talking to one of the men who carry the stretchers. Then he gives the stretcher man some paper money and walks towards the station entrance.

'Watch yerself,' someone shouts out, and a stretcher is carried past. There's a young man on it. He catches her eye and grins at her, lifting his hand to wave. Millie feels sick.

'Mumma, I'm frightened,' she says.

'Yes, let's get you out of here. We'll go to the café and wait there.'

'Will Papa be on a stretcher?'

'As far as I know, Millie, he's not injured. So I'm expecting him to walk from his train.'

When they get to the café there are chairs and tables outside, but still under the station roof. 'Sit here. Millie. I'll get us a drink. Don't move.'

Millie sits very still with her back to the station. She still feels sick, but, now that she's not looking at the stretchers, it's not so bad.

She watches the door for Mumma to return. Other people are sitting around her. Ordinary people like themselves. No one has a bandage. Some are reading papers, others chatting as if nothing was different in the world.

A man comes up and asks Millie if he might sit at the table. She looks at his khaki coat, but says she's sorry, that this table is taken and that he'll have to sit somewhere else. He thanks her very politely and goes to sit close by.

Millie starts to worry where Mumma is. She's taking a long time. She's been told not to move. But what if she's left alone in this horrible place?

For the first time she looks at the man who came to her table. He's sitting quietly and smiling at her. He's got the same warm smile as Papa, but he's thinner than Papa. She looks again and, as he opens his arms wide to her, she leaps from her chair and rushes to bury her face deep into his chest. She bursts into tears.

When Mumma arrives with a tray, to Millie she says, 'I told you not to move, young lady.' But Millie can see she's laughing. And to Papa she says, 'Welcome home, my darling.' Papa stands up and gently easing Millie away from him, takes the tray, puts it on the table and gives Mumma a big hug. She's smiling, but crying too.

'Why are we crying when we're happy?' Millie asks.

Papa picks her up. His eyes are brimming with tears too. 'Because happiness is as fierce an emotion as sorrow,' Papa says. 'And there's nothing wrong in showing a bit of emotion….and I'm so pleased to be home with my girls.'

'Daisy's with Martha making buns,' Millie tells him. She must tell Mary about the station. It's important information.

Mumma offers to get Papa a drink, but he says he'll share theirs and then they can go home. 'We must get this child away from this foul place.'

'I've never seen it like this,' says Mumma. 'And it makes you think.'

'I felt sick.'

'I think these poor souls feel a lot worse,' Papa says. 'Come on, let's get home and collect Daisy.'

Secrets

Millie wakes suddenly with a pain in her back. Daisy's always kicking her. She's still fast asleep, Millie can hear her breathing. She pushes Daisy gently, until she turns over with her face to the wall. Daisy mumbles, and settles back to sleep.

She can hear soft voices and remembers Papa's on leave. She lies listening to her parents. Her mother's voice is soft and gentle with that funny sound, lilting, Papa calls it. He's talking too, but she has to listen hard to hear. It's very dark, so they must be in bed in their own cupboard. Sleeping in a cupboard is good fun, she and Daisy are close to everyone, but hidden away too.

'My heart has let me down again, Flo. They won't let me serve on the front like Jack.'

'Well, that's good news for us. Will you stay in England?'

'No, I've done my work here. The horses are all recruited and trained, and all I have to do is see the poor creatures across to France.'

'What then?'

'Well, I shall stay there.'

'Doing what? Surely they could find you something to do here.'

Millie holds her breath, they're speaking much more quietly.

She thinks about getting up to use the chamber pot, but it will disturb her parents and she's happy lying in the dark listening to them. She keeps really still, but she can only hear odd words.

Papa's speaking. '…security services out in the country……back to the circus.'

'The circus?' Her mother this time.

''Sh-sh……secret…..joining a circus……listening in bars……..German spies……….know we're coming…'

'Can we contact you?'

'No ….. not safe….'

Her mother asks a question, but Millie can't hear.

'Acrobat……..animals, ponies,….'

There is more muffled talking and then much more clearly her father says, '… very secret, Flo. I shouldn't have told you really, but we promised to trust each other. You must never breathe a word to a soul.'

They're whispering again. Mumma giggles. Millie remembers the excitement of the day, meeting Papa, and going home to pick up Daisy. With her little sister hanging around his neck, Papa had given Martha a big hug and a kiss, and asked her about Grandad and Joe. He'd told Martha that he'd seen Joe recently at the training camp, and said, 'He's a fine young man, Martha. You must be very proud of him.' And then he'd held Martha's arm and looked into her eyes as if he wanted to say something, but couldn't. And she'd said, 'You're a good man, Frank. Welcome home.'

Later they'd all gone for a walk to the park. Like everyone else at home from the army, Papa had worn his uniform. Millie had taken the skipping rope Papa had given her at Christmas and had shown him how well she could skip now. He'd told her she was as light as a feather on her feet. He'd carried Daisy on his shoulders and Daisy had kept taking his cap off. Papa had told her he'd put her down if she didn't stop because if the King saw him without his cap, he'd be court-martialled. Millie remembers now that she was going to ask Papa what court-martialled meant, but she'd been so happy she'd forgotten.

They'd gone home and had a lovely tea of ham and potatoes and carrots, and trifle for pudding. It was much better than the plain bread they sometimes had. And Papa had read her another chapter from *Treasure Island*. The one where Jim is in the apple barrel and hears the pirates plotting against the Captain. Although she's heard this story lots of times, it's the first time she realises that Jim is a spy.....

When she wakes the next morning, Millie wonders if she'd dreamt hearing Mumma and Papa talking. But if the things she'd heard are true, then they are too secret for Mary to know. Perhaps she'll tell Mary about Jim in the apple barrel, listening to the pirates.

The Little Acrobat

The week at home with Papa is great fun. And Millie doesn't have to go to school.

But on Wednesday, Mumma has to go to the theatre for a rehearsal. 'I'm sorry, Frank,' she says. 'Mr Albert has told us we must be there.'

Papa says it doesn't matter. 'I want some time with my best girls. Anyway, we're going to the park to fly our kites. It's a good, windy day.'

On Tuesday, he'd helped Millie and Daisy to each make a diamond shape with thin bits of wood and brown paper. To these they'd tied short pieces of string decorated with little brown paper bows. Papa had to help Daisy, but Millie made her kite, all on her own.

'Good,' Papa had said. 'Now for the tricky part.' He'd taken a whole ball of string and wound string around the four corners of Daisy's kite. Millie'd watched carefully and, with her own ball of string, followed his every move. 'Well, these look very professional,' Papa had said. 'Let's see if we can brighten them up a bit.'

He'd found a small pot of red paint on the landing and, outside in the courtyard, they'd painted faces on the kites. 'For goodness sake, don't get any paint on your clothes. Your mother will never forgive me.' But at the end they'd all stood back proudly to admire their work.

Now the kites are propped against the wall by the door, waiting for their test flight.

Just before she leaves them, Mumma looks out at the sky, 'Don't get wet then,' she says.

And she'd been right. By 10 o'clock, the sky had darkened, and now it's raining hard.

'Bother,' says Papa. 'I was looking forward to seeing if our kites would fly, perhaps this afternoon.'

'Mumma can see them fly then,' Millie says.

Daisy likes that idea. 'Mumma see,' she shouts and dances around the room. Papa and Millie laugh at her.

Papa makes them cocoa and they have squashed fly biscuits. 'You can have squashed fly biscuits if you like,' says Papa. 'But I'm going to have a Garibaldi.'

'They're the same thing,' Millie says.

'Who said that?' Papa asks, and looks around the room, and they all laugh.

'I knew a Garibaldi once, and he wasn't a biscuit,' Papa says. 'He was an acrobat.'

'What's an ac-ro-bat?' Daisy asks.

'It's a man who can do all sorts of somersaults and handstands,' Millie tells her. 'Acrobats work at the theatre.'

'Yes, that's right,' Papa says. 'But, hundreds of years ago, they really began working in the travelling fairs and, of course, they're important acts in circuses, which is where I met, Mr Garibaldi.'

'In a circus?' Millie asks, and Papa nods. 'Would you like to hear the story of how I met Mr Garibaldi?'

And sitting at the table, Papa tells them how he joined the circus.

'I was 16 years of age. I was a small boy for my age, but very agile. I was good at gymnastics at school, could climb the wall bars and vault over the wooden horse in the gymnasium. It was a boarding school. It was different to your school, Millie. I slept there at night as well as doing lessons there during the day.'

'Were you good at arithmetic and English too?' Millie asks.

'Yes, not bad. Not as good as my brother or sister, but I could do mental arithmetic, do sums in my head. And I was very good at music, I played the piano, and I could speak French and German really well. I was top of the class for those. In fact, I was so good, that I was allowed to study with the year above me, and the German and French teachers gave me special classes where I spoke French and German like I might when having a conversation with you now, or my friends at the pub.'

'Say something in German and French,' Millie says.

Papa thinks for a few moments and then says, *'Je suis le petit acrobate.'*

'What did you say?' asks Millie.

'*I am the little acrobat* in French. Now, what do you think I am saying when I say, *Ich bin der kleine Akrobaten?*'

'*I am the little acrobat?* Is that German?'

'Yes, quite right.'

Millie thinks about this. Daisy's finished her cocoa and has got down from the table to play with the dolls, taking Millie's doll and her own. Normally Millie would've shouted at her, but there are other more important things to worry about than stolen dolls.

'Were you the little acrobat?' she asks.

'Yes, Millie. I was the little acrobat. That is how I met Mr Garibaldi. I joined the circus to be an acrobat, and he was the man in charge of the troupe of acrobats.'

Papa's smiling at her, but his eyes look serious, 'I was sixteen, and I ran away from school and from my family and joined the circus.'

'But why?'

'Because at the time it seemed like the right thing to do. It was an international circus. It toured France and Germany, Italy too. It came to Framlingham, the town where my school was, in Suffolk. I went to see it every day. I was never as alive as I was when I was watching the circus performers. And after the shows I'd go behind the scenes to look at the animals and meet the men and women who'd entertained the public.'

'What animals did you see?'

'See if you can guess.'

Millie thinks. 'Did the circus have dogs?' Papa nods. 'And did it have elephants?'

'Yes two, a mother and her calf. And we had a lion and a tiger. They were all looked after by the lion tamer, who was also one of the clowns. That's the thing about a circus, you have to do more than one job.'

'Did you look after any animals?'

'Yes,' says Papa. 'We'd always had horses at home, so my job was to look after the horses.'

'Is that why you're looking after horses in the war?'

'Yes, I suppose it is. I find horses to help the soldiers and then train them to do new things.'

Daisy's chatting away to the dolls and Millie gets down from the table and goes to stand by Papa. She holds his arm. It makes her feels safe, close to him.

'What did you have to do in the circus?'

'Anything and everything. That's what happens in a circus, you have to muck in.' He moves his chair back from the table and gently lifts Millie onto his lap.

'And it gave me a chance to see Europe at least. I could practice my French and my German and do the things I was really good at, look after the horses and be an acrobat. I was a small boy for my age and they called me Francois, the little acrobat.'

'And Mr Garibaldi was in charge of you?'

'Yes, and he taught me to do tumbles without hurting myself, how to balance on top of a human pyramid, there were six of us, and I stood right at the very top. There were three men on the bottom row, supporting two more men, who supported me. Mr Garibaldi taught me to somersault through the air, and later he let me work on the trapeze.'

'What up in the circus roof?' Millie is amazed.

Papa nods, 'I had never been so happy. I felt like a bird flying through the air. It looks much scarier than it really is. It's all to do with timing.'

Millie's thinking about this, when Papa says, 'And then I was allowed to be in charge of the horses too. I had to change my clothes quickly and come out looking very smart in white trousers and back boots and a red coat with long-tails. And I carried a long whip so I could guide the horses around the ring.'

'But you met Mumma in the music hall.'

'Yes, when I was twenty I'd had enough of touring in Europe. So I joined a troupe of acrobats that worked in the theatres. It was there that I met and fell in love with Mumma. She was so beautiful and had such a lovely voice.'

'Would you and Mumma like it if I ran away?' Millie asks.

'No, Millie, we wouldn't. We love you very much and you are only nine years old. And before you ask, of course, my parents were horrified when I wrote to tell them that I'd left school. And my teachers were none too pleased either. My brother, Jack, told me there'd been a dreadful row, and sadly, my parents haven't spoken to me since that time.'

Millie wants to ask much more, but Papa's got up to look out of the window. It's still raining. He bends down and picks up Daisy. 'What a good little girl you are!' he says. 'Both of you are wonderful girls. My best girls. Now, how about a game of dominoes?'

Millie is beating Papa and Daisy when Mumma arrives home. She's out of breath from running in the rain.

'Have you had a good morning? What did you do instead of flying your kites?'

Millie is about to say that Papa has been telling them about joining the circus, when she catches his eye and he puts a finger to his mouth. More secrets then.

'Oh, all sorts of things, drinking cocoa and eating Garibaldi biscuits,' she says.

'Thank you for looking after the girls,' Mumma says.

'My treat. But Flo, I think we need your help now. What's for lunch?'

News

Later in the week, Papa says, 'My sister, Kit, has asked if she might visit you and the girls, Flo. Would you mind?'

Mumma bangs a pan down on the table.

'Flo, don't be like that. It isn't Kit or Jack's fault that my parents are so intolerant and near-sighted. They're stuck in a previous age.'

'Why the sudden change of heart? Kit and Jack were so worried about us that they couldn't come to celebrate our wedding.'

Millie looks at her mother. Uh-ho, she's going to blow in a minute, and we'll all have to run for cover. It's always the same when Papa mentions his family.

'You're right, of course.' Papa is smiling and his voice is calm. 'But that wasn't their choice. Times have changed, and my parents have been left behind by events. There are much more important things happening in the world now.'

Mumma seems calmer.

'And don't forget, Flo, Kit paid for our honeymoon. Do you remember?'

'I won't be treated as a charity case, patronised. We get by, we manage. Look at what we've achieved together.' She's angry again, and her eyes are full of tears. This is scary.

'Darling, that's not why Kit is coming. She wants to be a friend, whilst I'm away. To see you and the girls sometimes. She's joined up herself. She's going to come and work in Derby at the hospital. She'll need a friend too. Please, Flo. Be kind to her for me?'

Millie's holding her breath. Mumma gets up and starts to sort out the washing that's been hanging above the range on a rack. As she lowers it, the rack squeaks. Mumma's face is like thunder. Daisy, as if sensing trouble, has started to cry. Papa picks her up. He walks over to Mumma and says something quietly in her ear.

'Don't give me that blarney, Frank Elliot. I know your game and I won't be playing it, thank you very much.' She throws a pillow slip at him.

Millie lets her breath out in relief. It's over.

'Is your sister my aunt?' Millie asks her father later.

'Yes. Aunt Kit.'

'And is Jack, my Uncle Jack?'

'Yes.'

'Have I ever met them?'

'When you were a tiny baby.'

'Did they see Daisy when she was a tiny baby too?'

'No.'

'Why not?'

'For all sorts of reasons. All too complicated to answer. Now where's *Treasure Island*? Let's see what Jim's up to.'

And Millie thinks Mumma's quite right. Papa is clever. Clever at not answering questions.

She remembers that she was going to tell him about Mr Albert and what she'd seen. But she's so frightened of spoiling his time with them that she doesn't. Perhaps Ted had been right after all, perhaps she had imagined it. Or perhaps she should try and find out a bit more about what Mr Albert is up to. She likes that idea. And if Papa can have secrets, so can she.

Papa Goes Back to the Army

Almost as soon as Papa's arrived, he's gone again. Millie and Daisy clung to him before he left, but only he and Mumma went to the station.

As he was packing, Millie had given him a large picture of the four of them and had labelled it *The Elliot Family*. She'd drawn it on half of a theatre poster. She'd worked hard trying to get all the details right. Mumma's blouse, Daisy's curly hair, even her own horrible button boots. Papa's in his uniform wearing his cap. 'So you won't forget us,' she'd said. Papa had said he would never forget them and folded the paper very carefully so it would fit in the pocket inside his uniform jacket. 'Next to my heart.'

At Martha's, Millie and Daisy sit at the table and she puts some milk and broken biscuits in front of them. Millie watches Joe's Grandad who's sitting in his chair by the fire and is fast asleep. Martha follows her gaze. 'He was out and about last night on his wanderings. The police brought him home, I'm surprised they didn't wake you all up.' Millie smiles. Grandad is good at escaping, but Mumma has said that he always goes to the station or the park to march up and down like a soldier, so Martha, Joe and the police usually know where to find him.

Millie's been looking forward to telling Martha about meeting Papa at the station and about all the soldiers with their red bandages. But she spots a new photograph on Martha's mantelpiece, of Joe in his uniform. It's in a wooden frame and beside it is a tiny vase of flowers and a pile of letters. She helps Daisy to drink her milk instead.

She does tell Martha about Aunt Kit and how she's coming to see them.

'That'll be nice,' Martha says. 'You're mother will love that.' And Millie wonders why she hadn't sounded as though she meant it.

Interlude 1

Footsteps are crossing the wooden floor.

A key is turned in a lock. And there's a squeak as the heavy door to the cupboard opens.

Now the little acrobat feels as if he's flying in his box with the other lead figures. Wrapped in his crinkly tissue paper, he's quite safe.

He's going on a journey. Wherever he finds himself, he knows now that his time is almost here.

Act 2
Aunt Kit

Yesterday, after school, Millie had stayed out in the sunshine with her friends, Mary and Freda. They'd walked home through the park past the pond quacking at the ducks, and had fun running around the trees. She'd been hungry when she'd got home and hoped Mumma had made a cake.

'Well, aren't we the fortunate ones,' Mumma had said when Millie walked in. Putting her bag in the tiny entrance hall, Millie'd looked at the clock on the wall. Had she been very late? No, it hadn't been Millie Mumma was cross with this time. The bread and jam were still on the table and Daisy was munching happily. But Mumma hadn't been happy.

'I'll just wash my hands,' Millie'd said.

'Good girl.'

When she'd got back, she'd still kept well out of Mumma's reach, walking around the table to sit opposite Daisy who was grinning at her. Normally she might have stuck out her tongue at her sister, but not today.

Mother had been holding a letter in her hand. 'Her ladyship is coming tomorrow,' she'd said.

Oh, so that was it. 'Do you mean Aunt Kit?' Millie'd asked.

'Yes, of course I do. Who else would it be? The Queen of Sheba?'

So after school today, Millie's hurried home. She'd said good-bye to her friends at the school gate and, although she misses walking back with them, she doesn't want to miss out on seeing Aunt Kit. As she skips along the pavement, she wonders what her father's sister will be like. She wonders too if she'll arrive home to find the pots and pans flying around the room, Daisy cowering in the corner.

She climbs the stairs, goes to their front door and listens. There's no shouting. Daisy isn't crying. Just gentle voices. Quietly she opens the door and peers in.

Mumma and a lovely lady are sitting at the table. Daisy's sitting on the lady's knee. The lady is younger than Mumma. There's tea and cake on the table and a huge bunch of flowers, yellow and white roses and blue cornflowers, in the large brown jug.

The lady smiles warmly at Millie and says, 'Oh, my goodness. Hello Millie. You're beautiful like your mother, but you have your father's eyes. Was it good at school today?'

'Come on, child. Don't hang back,' Mumma says. She's smiling. 'Come and meet your Aunt. We've all been looking forward to meeting her, haven't we? She's been telling us of all the tricks your father got up to as a boy.'

Millie's still not sure. But Mumma does seem as if she's enjoying Aunt Kit's visit. Mumma puts out her hand to Millie to encourage her to join them, and Millie goes over to stand by her mother, holding onto her arm for security.

Aunt Kit smiles at Millie. 'It's really so special to meet you at last, Millie. If this awful war has done one thing, it's brought us together. I hope we'll be friends, you and I.'

Millie looks up at her mother. Is that going to be OK? That

Aunt Kit and Millie can be friends. Will Mumma allow it? Mumma is smiling.

'Aunt Kit has joined as a VAD, a nurse helper, at the local military hospital, Millie. Papa had said she would be in Derby, do you remember? But this is much closer.'

'That was the original plan, Florence…..'

'Frank always calls me Flo, as did my father. Please Kit, please do call me Flo.'

Millie's amazed. Is this the Mumma who'd been cross with Papa and in a terrible temper yesterday, muttering and grumbling about Aunt Kit's visit?

'Thank you. The original plan – Flo – was for me to work in Derby, but then I realised that it might take forever to get to see you all. I know I'll be busy and have to work long hours, but in Derby, even on a rare day off, I might not have time to reach you. Getting a place in Nottingham seemed the only answer. They need so much help all over the country, they were happy to let me change my plans.'

'Will you be looking after the soldiers without legs and arms?' Millie asks.

'Oh, yes. And those who have head wounds too. So many men have been hurt at the Front.'

Millie is about to tell her that Papa isn't fighting, but remembers this is a secret and she isn't supposed to know it. Instead she tells her aunt about meeting her father at the station.

'Will you mind the smell?' she asks.

But Mumma says, 'Millie, it's time you had your tea. You must be very hungry. Run and wash your hands and then sit opposite Aunt Kit. You can get to know each other better whilst I make another pot?'

As she eats, Mumma and Aunt Kit chat on about Papa. From where she sits Millie's able to look at her aunt. Grown-ups like to say who they think you look like. Often, Millie had wanted to shout, 'I look like me!' Aunt Kit had said she was beautiful like Mumma, but that she has Papa's eyes. And, looking now at Aunt Kit, she understands. Her aunt does look like her father, but not like the Farnsworth twins in her class, you can't tell them apart unless they have their cards, with their names, hanging around their neck. Perhaps it's her smile.

Aunt Kit has the same dark hair as Papa, cut quite short, straight, in a bob. Beside her on the table is a pretty white hat with flowers, with a small white bag on a satiny cord and white lace gloves. She's wearing a summer dress with white and grey stripes and there's lace on the shoulders. And a single string of white beads hangs around her neck.

Millie watches her Aunt. If Kit isn't used to their ways, she isn't letting on. And listening to her she realises that Aunt Kit speaks in the same way as Papa. No accent. She's a real lady, very polite, interested without being nosy.

And then she sees it. How you would know Papa and Aunt Kit were brother and sister. Aunt Kit had noticed that Millie was watching her and had caught her eye and given her a little crooked grin. Just like Papa. And she'd tilted her head in the funny way he does.

Now she gives Millie a wide smile. 'What have you seen?' she asks gently.

'Something Papa does,' Millie replies.

'I saw it too,' says Mumma. 'You both have a quizzical teasing look. Tip your head to one side.' And they laugh together.

'Do you know,' Millie says. 'Papa told me that he was the little acrobat.'

'Millie,' says Mumma. 'What are you saying?'

'It's true, Mumma. He said *Je suis un petit acrobat*. That's French. And he said *Ich bin der kleine Akrobaten*. That's German. He told me he ran away to work with Mr Garibaldi. He told me that day we were going to fly our kites, but it rained.'

'Oh, Kit.' Mumma says. 'This must be very painful for you. I am so sorry.'

'Why is it painful?' Millie asks.

Mumma has stopped smiling. 'Millie, you'll be sent to bed if you persist.'

'Flo,' Aunt Kit puts her hand over Mumma's. 'It's alright, really it is.' And to Millie she says, 'Mumma is worried that I may be sad talking about Papa running away to the circus. It was a terrible time for us all. He was very young and left a wonderful school. His teachers were very upset, but it hurt my parents most of all. My father had plans that Papa would follow him into the family business, a shoe factory in Norwich. Frank didn't want that life, despite my parents' plans for him. Jack and I didn't like his going either, but we understood. Frank was following a dream.'

And then Aunt Kit says, 'But Flo, isn't Millie clever? Did you hear how she remembered what Frank had said in French and in German?'

'Why was he following a dream?' Millie asks.

'Didn't he tell you about the toy circus we all used to play with?'

Millie shakes her head.

'We had this toy circus and it was Frank's favourite toy. We all enjoyed it, but it was Frank who played with it most. He used to look at the smallest acrobat and say, 'One day I will be the little acrobat and turn somersaults in a big top with thousands of people cheering me on.'

Turning again to Mumma, she says, 'Flo, do you mind? I've taken a huge liberty and brought it for the girls. If you'd rather they didn't have it, I would quite understand, but as they're now the little ones in the family, perhaps they could have some fun with it?'

Aunt Kit bends down and from under the table, she draws out a large cotton bag. Inside are two brown boxes.

Mumma says, 'You're very lucky girls to have such a wonderful toy. What do you say to Aunt Kit?'

Millie and Daisy say thank you and both give Aunt Kit a kiss on the cheek. Daisy makes them all laugh by giving Aunt Kit a huge hug too which almost strangles her.

'May we play with it now?' Millie asks.

'No,' says Mumma. 'I think we should give all our attention to Aunt Kit, and the circus will distract you. She can't stay long.'

'Will you take care of it? It's quite old and precious. It belonged to one of your great-aunts and she gave it to Papa when he was a boy. We loved playing with it so much that it's really quite battered now, but there's still lots of playing left in it.'

Then Mumma tells Kit about their work in the music hall and Kit says she would like to come to a performance sometime.

'You can sit on the basket in the wings with me,' Millie offers. 'Ted has found a purple cushion and there's loads of room.'

'I think Aunt Kit would prefer a seat in one of the boxes, Millie,' Mumma says.

'You know, Flo, if there's space on the basket with Millie, I'd just love that. Much more exciting than sitting out front.'

It's agreed and Millie feels a tickle of happiness. Their little family has grown. Now they are five. She asks Mumma if she can get down from the table and goes to fetch *Treasure Island* to show her Aunt.

'Oh, my goodness. Your Papa loved this book as a boy. Have you seen that at the front it says he won it as a prize at school?'

Millie nods. 'He still loves it, I think. He reads it to me every time he comes home. I know the story so well I can remember it by looking at the pictures, but I can read the words too.'

'Does he still do the funny voices for the pirates?'

They laugh as Millie says he does, and Aunt Kit gives her a little hug.

As Aunt Kit gets ready to leave them, she says she would like to see them all again very soon if they would allow.

'Perhaps if this weather holds, we could have a picnic in the park?'

And they all agree that it is a lovely idea.

'Then I can show you how I can skip,' Millie says.

The Toy Circus

After Aunt Kit has gone and they've cleared away, Mumma says that they may look at the circus for a little while before bedtime. But they must sit at the table.

The two brown cardboard boxes have large black fancy writing on them. The flat one says *Circus Rings* and the other deeper box says *Circus Animals and People*. Each is held together with string that crosses in the middle. Mumma tells Daisy not to pick at the paper tape on the corner of a box. 'It's there to keep the old boxes in shape,' she says.

Very carefully they remove the string. Then they open the flat box. Inside is a wrinkled piece of paper. Mumma lays it out carefully on the table. It was white once, but now it's a dark creamy colour, and as she lifts it up, it almost falls into four pieces. There's faded writing on it. Underneath are three wooden rings, each the size of dinner plates which fix together in a shape like a clover leaf. A trefoil, Mumma says.

'You have rings like this for your embroidery,' Millie says.

'Yes, they do look similar, but they're different, Millie. Can you see how these slot together? And there are little doors at the side to let the circus acts enter the rings and move between them.'

Inside the other box everything has been carefully wrapped in creamy-white tissue paper. Millie puts her nose into the box and sniffs. 'It smells funny. Like it's very old and 'metally', like the drawer with the knives and forks.'

Daisy has started to pull at the paper. 'Let's try and keep the paper to use again later,' Mumma suggests. 'So don't tear it please, Daisy. You must be very gentle.'

Very carefully, they unwrap the heavy little parcels. Millie thinks again about Aunt Kit. After they'd made plans for their picnic, she'd said that she needed to get back to the hospital and hoped they'd enjoy playing with the circus. They'd all said good-bye and Aunt Kit asked if she might give them all a kiss. Millie thought her aunt smelled of roses. Having an Aunt Kit was very good.

'Shall I come down with you?' Mumma had asked.

'I'll be just fine,' Aunt Kit had said and had given Mumma a hug.

'Lion,' Daisy shouts and bangs it on the table. It makes a small dent in the wood.

Millie is very cross and shouts at her. 'Don't, you'll break it.'

Mumma says, 'Daisy, you must be careful. I'm not sure you're old enough to play with this yet? Perhaps we could open the packets together.' She takes Daisy onto her knee.

'I've found a clown,' says Millie.

'And we've found a horse,' Mumma says.

'And I've found Papa's little acrobat!' The little figure is dressed in a tight, single costume of white, just like he's wearing the thick leggings and long sleeved vests men wear in the winter. Over this there is a large pair of shiny blue satin bloomers with gold stars on them, with a little waistcoat to match. And he wears blue slippers with straps on his feet.

There are so many little parcels that it takes quite a while to open every one of them, but in the end they look proudly at their finds laid out on the table.

'It feels like we've been on a treasure hunt,' Millie says. 'But with this we knew where to look, not what we'd find.'

Mumma agrees. 'And this is real treasure. Papa has played with all of these little animals and people, so they are very precious to us, aren't they?'

'And Aunt Kit,' said Daisy.

Mumma laughs, 'Yes, and Aunt Kit.'

They look at all the little figures laid out on the table before them. There's a ring master in a bright blue coat, a tall hat and holding a long whip. There are four acrobats in shiny pantaloons, and three clowns in baggy clothes. There's a strong man dressed in a tiger skin which hangs over one shoulder, and he has black tights, and holds up his heavy arms so you can see his muscles.

Millie holds the strong man in her hand. 'He's very heavy,' she says.

There's a lady in a pretty pink ballerina's dress; she's holding her thin arms out, but she's standing on the toes of one foot and her other leg is curved around behind her. Mumma says that she would ride around on a horse, making different dance shapes, but keeping her balance.

Millie finds a white horse with a flying mane that has a tiny little bit of metal on its back where the lady's foot fits. They fix the lady and the horse together.

'There, doesn't she look the part,' says Mumma.

'Uh-ho, broken,' says Daisy holding up a tiger. It has only one ear, but all four of its legs and a long tail. It's snarling as tigers do, but they see that the paint on the side of the tiger had worn away and the dark grey metal is showing through.

'It's fine,' Mumma says. 'But this is exactly why we have to be careful. The figures are so old that they can break easily or the paint might come off. So now we have to make up a story about why the tiger lost his ear or keep pretending that it's still there.'

There are two tigers and a pride of four lions, one male and three females. There are two large elephants and a young calf elephant that is standing on a drum. There are three more horses and four dogs, one with a ball on its nose.

Millie puts the ring master in one ring with the elephants, and Daisy puts the clowns in another.

'You put something in,' Millie says to Mumma, and Mumma puts the horses in the final ring.

'Have we put Papa in the circus?' Millie asks. She looks at the mounds of paper on the table. The little acrobat is lying on his side with his face to one of the box lids. 'Oh, you've toppled over,' she tells him, and stands him up in the ring with Mumma's horses. 'There that's better. Now you're like Papa. A little acrobat in charge of the horses.'

'Did Papa tell you that he worked on the trapeze, flying high up above the crowds, at the top of the big tent?' Millie nods. 'Wasn't he brave? I couldn't have done that. But I don't think this circus has a trapeze.'

'If you write to Papa, can I draw a picture of the circus please?' Millie asks.

'Me draw too,' shouts Daisy.

They all think that this is an excellent idea and, looking at the circus together, they wonder what Papa is doing.

Interlude 2

From his place beside the horses, the little
acrobat looks around. He takes in the poorly
furnished room, the woman and the two girls.
This is a different family, in different
circumstances, but so many things are the same.

And he knows now that his wait is over.

By the time they've cleared away, and washed and changed, ready for bed, Daisy is crying and holding her tummy. Mumma feels her forehead and says she feels hot. Millie is just getting a book for a story, when Daisy starts to heave. Mumma grabs a bowl and rushes her out to the toilet.

When they get back, Daisy is smiling. 'Me sick,' she says.

'You ate too much cake,' Millie tells her.

'Well that's as maybe,' says Mumma. 'But I think to be on the safe side Daisy should sleep with me tonight.'

Lying in bed, Millie feels guilty because Daisy isn't well, but having the bed to herself is a treat, no kicks, no arm flung across her face to wake her up. And she's taken the little acrobat to bed with her. She likes him best of all. She'd slipped him into the pocket of her pinafore as they were putting the circus away. He was Papa's favourite too.

She holds the heavy little figure in her hand now, looking at it, wondering what Papa is doing. She smells the metal it's made of and, in the dim gas light, looks at the thick cracked paint.

Millie's feeling tired and decides to put the little man under her pillow, but before she does she gives him a kiss on the top of his head and whispers, 'Take my love to Papa, Acrobat.'

Millie finds herself surrounded by noise and bustle. She looks down and sees boxes and crates, waggons and horses, and hundreds of busy soldiers in khaki uniforms, shouting and calling below her.

She's high up on the deck of a ship looking out to the dock. There are cranes lifting whole waggons and large guns on wheels off the ship, putting them on the dock below. And as if it's flying through the air, a horse floats beside her. It's held in a large sling and is very scared, its eyes wide and its ears flicked back. But it too is lowered down on the ground, where the poor thing stands bewildered, before a soldier comes up and releases it to join others along by the high dock wall.

She sees Joe march down the gangplank with lots of other soldiers. Like them, he's in uniform and has a large pack on his back and is holding a real rifle. She waves and calls his name, but although he turns in her direction, as if sensing someone is looking at him, he doesn't see her.

Millie looks now at the little figure in her hand. She worries that she might drop it and tries to put it in her pocket, but realises she's in her long cotton nightdress. She holds onto it even tighter than before.

She has no shoes on her feet, and can feel the warm wood of the deck she stands on. And although the flags on the boat are blowing in the wind, she's sheltered in her corner of the deck. She can smell the sea, that salty, sea weedy smell that reminds her of the sandcastles she made when her parents were appearing in the summer show at Morecambe. They'd walked by the sea every day for the whole summer.

She's amazed by all the horses. She sees them put into pairs, each pair set to pull a waggon with casks and boxes. Some of the covered waggons have red crosses on them. Millie remembers the station and shivers. Other horses are pulling large guns. Horses are really patient animals. She can smell them too, would have known they were there even if she hadn't seen them. There's that sweet smell. Papa says it's their sweat mixed with a hint of muck. Best smell in the world, he reckons. He would.

One horse is scared and rears up on its hind legs, pawing the air with its hooves. Men scatter away from it like ants. It's beautiful, like a chestnut with a glossy black mane and tail. A man goes over to it. He's dressed as the other soldiers in uniform, but doesn't have a back pack or a gun. He catches hold of the rein and says something to the animal, whispering in its ear. It settles immediately.

Millie calls out as loudly as she can. 'Papa, Papa, up here. Look, it's me, Millie!' She's waving too, but Papa carries on attaching the horse to another cart. He pats it fondly on the rump as it moves away. 'Good lad, Chester,' he says.

Things are quieter now and Millie notices that the sailors on the ship are busy, washing the decks and tidying up. Perhaps they're getting ready to go home.

Papa comes up the gangplank and as he gets to the top, he salutes a tall man who has some gold on the shoulders of his uniform. He's saluting Papa and smiling at him.

'Are you ready, Elliot?'

'Yes, Captain.'

'Good man. You've done wonders with those terrified beasts. We'd have been very happy for you to follow them to the front, but we have more important work for you, as you know.'

'Yes, Sir.'

'It won't be easy. And it may be dangerous, but your language skills are of high order. No-one else could do the job. You're clear about what you have to do?'

'Yes, Sir. I'm to join the Circus Suisse in Bergerac as a general help and acrobat. Travelling with the circus, I'm to engage the locals in conversation and find out if there are any German spies operating in the Dordogne.'

'Quite right. The French need your language skills. Any final questions?'

'One thing I don't quite understand is, why Circus Suisse?'

'Oh, that's simple. Switzerland is a neutral country and as such the Swiss are not part of this war. No one will question why a young man from Switzerland isn't fighting at the front. They'll leave you alone. But you'll need to be vigilant, Elliot. This is top secret work, vital to the war effort. No-one likes a spy.'

Millie gasps. Papa will be doing special, dangerous work. He's going to be a spy.

The Captain is speaking again. 'Looks like your transport has arrived. You'll find a change of clothes and your kit under the bundles of hay. The old farmer will take you to a safe house to change and get yourself settled. Then he'll give you the papers and money you need for your journey down South.'

'Thank you, Sir.'

'Good luck, Elliot. You're a good and brave man.'

Millie watches as Papa and the Captain salute each other again.

She waves him goodbye, knowing now that he cannot see her, but wondering about what she's seen. She looks at the little figure in her hand. She can hardly see it because her eyes have filled with tears. She gives it a kiss on the top of its head and says, 'Keep Papa safe, Acrobat.'

Millie is back in her bed. The gas light is glimmering above her and she looks at the little figure. She tucks it under her pillow. She'll have to be careful that Mumma doesn't find out that she's taken it. She lies for a minute listening to Mumma singing to Daisy and wonders about what she's seen. Papa is a spy in France. That's a big secret. She pulls the little brass chain to turn off the gas mantle, turns over, tugs the sheet and blankets up to her chin, and falls fast asleep.

Act 3

The Picnic

Aunt Kit is putting cold sausages, a huge pork pie and tomatoes out onto the large white tablecloth that Mumma has thrown over the blankets they're all sitting on. Mumma's brought home-made bread spread with butter, and ham, cheese, cucumber and pickle too. Finally Aunt Kit takes a large bowl of strawberries out of her basket and a jar of cream.

'Yummie,' says Daisy, jumping up to walk across the tablecloth towards the strawberries.

'No, you don't, young lady,' Mumma says as she grabs Daisy, lifting her high in the air and sitting her on the rug beside her. 'Sit like Millie. Look, she's being very good with her legs crossed.'

Daisy tries to cross her legs and kicks over the bowl of tomatoes.

'Be careful,' Millie shouts. 'You're so clumsy.'

'Well, this looks good, I must say,' says Aunt Kit as she pops the tomatoes back into the bowl. 'I should say it's fit for the King'.

They're sitting under a huge old tree and Millie can see right across the park. A new group of soldiers are practising marching. The new recruits have uniforms now and wooden guns. She can hear the Sergeant-Major barking out his orders, but not what he's saying. She can see the men trying to keep their lines straight and they get in an awful muddle when they have to turn around and march back the other way, and bump into each other. The Sergeant-Major stamps his foot. Millie laughs. Mumma tells her to shush. 'It isn't polite to laugh at other people.' But Mumma and Aunt Kit are smiling at the soldiers too.

Above her in the tree, the birds are singing and she looks up through the leaves at the blue sky with white clouds which are moving very slowly. Papa would've loved it here. Joe too, and wonders what he's doing.

Aunt Kit is looking at her. 'I wonder if your Papa is enjoying such a lovely day. You know I was thinking of him sitting somewhere thinking of all of us, thinking of him.'

'Like the Hall of Mirrors at the fair,' Mumma says. 'You see your reflection over and over again, and our thoughts and love are probably going backwards and forwards across the Channel.'

'Flying over the white cliffs of Dover,' says Aunt Kit.

Millie sees Mr Albert in the trees behind the new soldiers. He's writing notes again in his black book, and he's counting, pointing his pencil in the direction of the soldiers, almost as if he's adding them up...one, two, three.... Millie's sure now that what he's doing is bad. Why else would he hide and spy on the soldiers? She shivers. The Captain said that no-one likes a spy.

Mumma and Aunt Kit are talking about the hospital. Millie jumps up. She's going to run down to the trees behind Mr Albert and see if she can see what he's writing in his book. She's not gone far when Mumma calls her back.

'I won't be long,' Millie says. 'I just want to see how long it takes me to run down the hill and back.'

Mumma is not pleased. 'Do as you're told, for once in your life.'

'Sor-ry,' Millie says and flops down by the picnic again.

Aunt Kit is smiling. 'You look like you've got ants in your pants, child?'

Even Mumma thinks that's funny. And by the time they've all stopped laughing, Mr Albert has gone. But Millie has a plan now. She needs to see that notebook. What is it Mr Albert is writing down and giving to the man with the bowler hat?

As she eats strawberries and cream, Millie looks out over the park. She sees men in blue uniforms, some are in wheelchairs being pushed by nurses, enjoying the sunshine. She's getting used to seeing men who are injured now. Some have no legs, and they sit in wheel chairs, their empty trouser legs turned up and held with large silver safety pins, others have no arms. Some walk with crutches and sticks.

But there are men and women too who don't seem to be part of the war, walking with children who run ahead and play.

'Oh, here we go,' says Aunt Kit. 'Here comes the White Feather Brigade.'

Millie stands for a better look. Three women are walking through the park. They look very tall in their long grey skirts and white blouses. They have long hair tied up under large hats. Across their shoulders they wear a purple ribbon.

'What's the White Feather Brigade?' Millie asks.

'Women who should know better,' says Mumma. 'Self-righteous prigs.'

Aunt Kit laughs. 'Well, there are many who would agree with

you, Flo. They're women who believe that every able man should be fighting for their country. And if they meet a young man who's not in uniform they present him with a white feather. They're saying, 'You are a Coward.''

Before Millie can ask what a coward is, Mumma says, 'That's someone whose not brave, doesn't do their duty.'

The Captain had said Papa was good and brave. But not every young man is a coward, some of them just aren't well enough to fight, like Ted.

'How do they know who's a coward? The men who are injured can't fight, so it wouldn't be right to give them a white feather.'

'Ah, that's easy,' Aunt Kit explains. 'The men who've been injured in the war all wear a blue uniform. It tells the rest of us that they are still in the army, but that they are too hurt to fight.'

'Will they go back to fight when they're better?' Millie asks.

'Only those who can walk and use both of their arms. The rest will no longer have to fight.'

'Finished,' shouts Daisy and holds out her hands to be wiped clean of strawberry juice.

'Good girl,' Mumma says. 'Now off you go both of you and have a little play whilst Aunt Kit and I pack up.'

One of the women has marched away from her friends and is handing a white feather to a young man. He doesn't want to take it and turns away from her. She sticks it in the top pocket of his jacket and gives him a push.

Perhaps they should give a white feather to Mr Albert and he'd have to go to war and stop watching people.

Spying

'Oh, look at the ducklings,' Freda says. 'There are eight there. They're so-o sweet.'

Millie, Mary and Freda are dawdling home through the park. They can hear the shouted commands of the Drill Sergeant. There must be some more new soldiers.

'Me brother signed up yesterday,' Freda tells them. 'Me Mam burst into tears when he told her. She screamed at him, 'You never were very bright. What you want to do that for?' But he said he was doing it for King and country. Still, she walloped him with the tin tray and it took ages to get the dent out.'

'Martha was the same,' says Millie. 'Her Joe was too young to join up really. But he did join and she screamed too when he told her. And dropped a plate.'

Mary says, 'If your Alf signed up yesterday, he'll be practising here this afternoon, won't he? Let's go and look.'

The girls run off to the big open space of green used by the new soldiers. And yes, there are the new recruits learning to march.

'Where's your Alf?' Mary asks.

'He's the tall one over there at the back.'

'He's very handsome,' says Mary, and they all giggle.

As the soldiers walk past them, Millie sees Mr Albert behind them, hiding in the trees, where he was when they had the picnic. He's watching and has his book open.

'Stay there,' Millie says to her friends. 'I'll be back soon.' And before they can ask more or follow her, Millie runs around the soldiers and into the woods behind Mr Albert.

Using the Sergeant's voice, as he barks out commands, to find her way, she moves through the trees until she comes up behind Mr Albert. He's busy and hasn't heard her. He's counting – thirteen, fourteen, fifteen – and making notes in his book.

Millie starts to talk as she walks up to him. 'Hello, Mr Albert,' she says.

Mr Albert snaps his books shut and drops his pencil. As he picks it up, he turns to look at Millie. His face is full of fear, but soon it changes. He goes very red, and he growls at her.

'What are you doing here, urchin?'

Millie's frightened now. She'd thought he'd be pleased to see her, like he is at the theatre. She hadn't thought he'd be cross. Her plan had been to say Hello and talk to him to try and find out what he's doing.

'Clear off!' he says. But it is he who moves away, back into the trees. Millie watches as he starts to run and stumble through the little wood.

The Sergeant is looking in their direction and Millie decides to walk out towards the open space, the soldiers and back to her friends. Her heart is thumping.

'You, OK?' the Sergeant asks.

Millie nods. 'Yes, thank you.' But she doesn't feel OK, she wants to get home. The Sergeant watches her as she skips round to her friends.

'Where you been?' they ask.

'Oh, just to see someone I know. But it wasn't him.' She bends over, hands on her knees, to catch her breath which seems to have disappeared.

'You alright?' Freda asks. 'You look like you're ill.'

Mary says, 'Did you hear that Johnny Hanley's Dad is missing in action? They haven't had a letter in ages. Me Mam says that's awful, 'cos you don't know what's happened. The family don't know what to think.'

'He was very quiet at school today. That must be why,' Millie says. 'I'd hate that.'

'You 'eard from your Dad lately?' Freda asks.

'Yes,' Millie lies. The others are talking about their father's letters. Mary's very excited about hers. 'Me Dad got a mate to write his letter, but he signed it himself.'

Millie's had enough and needs to think. Shouting 'Bye,' she runs off home.

Worries

Mumma looks up as Millie bangs through the door. 'Hey, what's up with you, young lady?' Mumma puts down her sewing and gets up from her chair.

Millie is close to tears. 'We haven't had a letter from Papa since he was at home. Freda and Mary's fathers write to them. It was only me and Johnny Hanley who didn't have letters today. And his Dad's missing in action. Thought dead, that means, doesn't it. And Papa's doing secret stuff, so he can't write. And I mustn't tell anyone, must I?'

'Goodness! What a lot of worries for such a young girl.' Mumma takes Millie by the hand and they go back to Mumma's chair. Millie is lifted onto her lap. Daisy's drawing pictures with chalk and a slate at the table. She waves at Millie and pulls a funny face and Millie has to smile at her.

'Most importantly, we don't know what Papa is doing, but we know he can't write and tell us. And we can't talk about it because we don't know.'

'But I heard him tell you that what he was doing is secret and he said about a circus.'

'Did he?' Mumma seems surprised. Now Millie's not sure if she remembered what Papa had said to Mumma, or whether she saw it when she was on the boat. Perhaps it was a dream, after all?

'I think it's very sad about Johnny Hanley's father. I wonder if there is anything we can do to help his mother?'

Millie tells Mumma about Freda's brother Alf and how they'd been to watch him learning to march. 'His Mum hit him over the head with a tin tray, she was so cross with him.'

Mumma laughs and gives Millie a hug. 'Now,' she says. 'How about some tea for you and then perhaps you and Daisy would like to play with the circus. If Miss Daisy is very careful.' Millie knows that Mumma's trying to cheer her up and gives her a kiss, getting another hug in return.

Trouble

They've had a good game with the circus and Daisy's been very careful. She's been in charge of the horses. It's left Millie to put the lions in one ring and the clowns and acrobats in the other. She lets Daisy play at being the ringmaster.

They're just packing it away again when there's a loud banging on their door. As Mumma goes to open it, she says, 'This poor door is having a hard time today, first Millie….'

As she opens the door Martha barges through. 'And now Martha…Martha, whatever's the matter?'

Martha's sobbing and shouting, waving a piece of paper in the air. 'It's your fault, Florence Elliot. All your fault.' She walks up to Mumma and gives her a push on the shoulder, waving the paper in her face. 'You and your la-de-da ways, filling a young boy's head with ideas. Well, clever old you, think yourself lucky he's only critically injured. He's not dead like some you wrapped your charms around. But my lovely boy will never walk again. I expect you're feeling mighty proud of yourself. Irish stock, killing our English boys.'

Millie's frightened and Daisy has started to cry. There's a great banging on their ceiling and from above them they hear shouts about people needing sleep. Millie puts Daisy into their bed cupboard and picks up the rest of the circus and takes it with her. She gives Daisy a hug and tells her not to cry. 'It's alright,' she coos.

But Martha is still yelling at Mumma. 'And don't think I'll be able to look after those brats of yours, whilst you go to send good men to their deaths. When my Joe comes home, I'll have enough on my plate with him and Grandad.'

Millie can't see what's going on, but she hears Mumma now, her voice quite loud at first. 'Martha, Martha, what terrible news. You must be devastated. Joe's a wonderful boy. He's no coward, braver than most.' Mumma is still talking, but her voice is a little softer. 'It's terrible news, Martha. I'm so sorry. Sit down, my dear.'

There's the sound of a bottle being opened. 'I think a drop of brandy wouldn't go amiss.' More grumbling from Martha, but she's settling down now.

'May I see the letter?' Mumma again.

'Oh my dear, it says he is on his way back to Nottingham. That's wonderful news. Let's hope you can get him home soon. But we must ask Kit to look out for him.'

Some more grumbling. 'And you're right, Martha. It's a terrible thing to be helping recruit these boys and I've decided to stop doing it. The girls need me and I have prevailed upon your kindness too long. Perhaps we can help you in return.'

Millie is sad about Joe, but is trying not to bounce up and down at the news that they will have Mumma with them more. She gives Daisy a hug and Daisy doesn't let go.

A Secret Mission

Millie looks out of the window. The sun is shining and she can hear children outside.

'Can I go and play?'

'Not this morning, Millie. I need you to run an errand for me,' Mumma says, as she goes out to the landing.

Bother. Millie slumps in a chair, her knees up under her chin. It's not fair. Daisy looks up at her, but doesn't come over.

'Whatever's the matter with you?' Mumma says, when she gets back. 'Get yourself off that chair and go and get dressed.'

'I don't want to go shopping. I want to play out. Look at the sunshine.'

'Who said anything about shopping? Get a move on child, or you'll be late.'

'I don't want to do any errand. I want to go and play.'

'But, you'll want to come to the theatre on Friday with Aunt Kit, I suppose? And you won't be doing that if you don't help me. So, get a move on.'

'Now,' says Mumma. 'I think you're old enough to help me with this today. If you don't want to do it, perhaps I could go myself, and you can take Daisy shopping instead.'

This is different.

'I need you to go to the theatre with a message for Mr Albert. He's asked me to think of people who might take over from me when I leave at the end of the season. And I've got a few names here. The sooner we can get them to him, the sooner I can make plans to leave.'

'I can do that, Mumma.' This is really exciting, much better than playing.

'He's auditioning this morning, so he'll be in the theatre. Remember the rules, Millie. Just give him this piece of paper and come home.'

Mumma helps Millie finish her hair and put on her hat. 'It'll mean a tram ride, Millie. Do you think you will be able to do that?'

'I've done it plenty of times with you. The number 6 tram and I get off outside the theatre.'

'Good girl. Go straight there. And come straight back. Ask Ted to help you get back across the road. It's too busy to cross without help.'

As Millie skips down the stairs, Mumma calls, 'And hurry back. No dawdling now. And sit downstairs on the tram.'

'I will.'

The tram ride is fun on her own. When other children get on with grown-ups, Millie stares at them and then looks out of the window. Places she's seen on her tram trips with Mumma look different in the day light. When she gets to the theatre, Millie runs around to the stage door and rings the bell.

Ted opens it. 'Hello, Millie. Lovely to see you on this bright morning.' He sticks his head out of the door and looks up at the sky.

'When I've finished, could you take me across the road, please?'

'Sure can. Come and find me.'

Millie dawdles through the corridors towards the stage area. Everything is very quiet. She passes Mr Albert's office and notices that his jacket is hanging over the back of the chair behind his desk. She looks through the crack in the door. He's not in the office.

She walks down to the stage and sees men sitting on a line of chairs. Ted joins her. 'New comedians. Basil joined up last week and we need a replacement fast.'

She hears Mr Albert. 'Thank you. Don't call us, we'll call you.' And a man comes off the stage holding his hat and looking sorry for himself.

Mr Albert calls, 'Next.' And the next man in line gets up and walks towards the stage.

''Ow'd it go, mate?' Ted asks the man with the hat.

'Not bad.'

'Well, good luck. Now Millie, let's get you down to the big chief.' Ted lifts the heavy red curtain and Millie ducks underneath, walks down the stage steps and into the theatre. She sees Mr Albert sitting smoking a cigar, with a pile of papers on his lap. He's in his shirt and tie and has a band of silver above each elbow. Seeing her, he puts his hand up to stop the man on the stage. 'Be with you in a minute,' he calls.

She's been so excited about this errand that she's quite forgotten that the last time she saw Mr Albert was in the woods at the park. She takes a deep breath and holds out the paper

Mumma has given her.

'Mr Albert, Mumma asked me to bring you this.'

'Come and sit down next to me, Millie,' Mr Albert says. 'Watch these jokers with me.'

'Thanks, but this is my first time on a tram ride and Mumma says I must go straight home.'

Mr Albert looks at her. A look that goes on forever. He opens Mumma's sheet of paper and nods. 'Good,' he says. 'Off you go.' She's dismissed with a flap of his hand. 'As you were,' he shouts to the man on the stage.

Millie walks quickly back to the stage to find Ted waiting for her. She knows he's been looking out for her. 'Right, ready to go home?'

'Can I just go to the toilet?' Millie says

'Sure. Come and find me when you're finished.'

This is her only chance. She walks back in the direction of the toilet knowing that it will take her past Mr Albert's office. Nothing has changed. She looks both ways down the corridor and then steps into the office. The coat is still hanging over the back of the chair just as it had been when she'd first seen it. She tries all the pockets. The jacket smells of scent, but also sweat, like old clothes. She shivers. The pockets are gritty. The grit gets under her nails. There's a pencil, but no book. Perhaps he's got it with him. She's just about to give up when she remembers that men have pockets inside their jackets too.

There in the shiny jacket lining is a small pocket and putting her hand in she feels a little book. She pulls it out. She's just opening the book when the telephone rings. The bell is very loud and she jumps dropping the book. She hears steps coming along towards the office and dives under the desk. There's just enough room for her between the two sets of wooden drawers that hold the desk top.

Someone walks into the office. It's Ted. She can see his shoes and the frayed ends of his trousers.

''Ello. Mr Albert's office. Ted speaking'

Silence. Millie hardly dares to breathe.

'No, sorry mate, he's busy auditioning. Not to be disturbed. Do you want to leave a message?'

More silence. Millie stays like a statue.

'He'll be around this afternoon, you should be able to catch him then.'

She hears the click of the phone as the handset is replaced. 'Charming,' Ted says. 'Same to you with brass knobs on.' Millie daren't laugh. She watches as Ted's feet turn away from the desk and walk out of the door. She hears the door squeak as he pulls it behind him. Don't lock it please. She hears his steps going back down the corridor.

Her heart is pounding. She opens the book. Many of pages have been torn out, but on some that remain there are lots of numbers, and writing about different bits of the army. She comes out of her hiding place. Taking a pencil from the desk, carefully she tears a page out of the back of the book and copies some of the information.

28ᵗʰ May 1916

10 x 8 = 80 men

Drill sergeant from the North Notts Artillery (France)

Rifles

She folds the paper in half, puts it in her pocket, and places the little notebook back into the pocket where she found it. Then taking a deep breath, she steps back into the corridor. It's empty. She walks quickly back towards the stage to find Ted. There are only a few men sitting on the chairs now.

'Hello, lovely,' he says. 'I'd forgotten about you. Did you get lost?'

Millie just smiles. She follows Ted to the stage door and across the road. They have to dart between trams, lorries, horses and carts, and the odd car.

'Take care, Mill.'

'Bye, Ted. Thank you. See you on Friday.'

And he's gone with a wave. She can see him dodging back through the traffic. She stands at the tram stop waiting for the number 6 to take her home. In her pocket is the piece of paper from Mr Albert's notebook with the information she's copied down. It isn't very much and she already knew some of it. She, Mary and Freda could have counted the soldiers. Some people like to spot trains and write down their numbers in notebooks. Perhaps that's what Mr Albert is doing. Spotting new soldiers. But if so, why would he do it hidden from view in the trees? And why would he get money for the pages in his book?

Aunt Kit at the Theatre

Aunt Kit's promised trip to the theatre has arrived and she's sitting with Millie on the large wicker basket in the wings of the theatre. Around them is the usual backstage noise and chaos. They're having a great time together. Millie introduced Aunt Kit to Mr Albert and he bowed very low to her. 'We are most honoured,' he said. 'Frank Elliot's sister is always welcome to attend our little show, and obviously, dear lady, you should have a proper seat in the auditorium. As one of the nurses at the hospital, this is no place for you.'

Oh no! Millie wouldn't be allowed out front and would be separated from Aunt Kit. But Aunt Kit has been most firm on the matter. 'I know I'm in the way, but it's so exciting seeing the show from this angle. I've already learned so much, and it's clear that you run a very fine theatre, *Monsieur Albert.*'

Aunt Kit has pronounced Mr Albert's name as if he's French, but he isn't, Millie knows that. Mumma calls him Mister Albert in a very English way, to annoy him. 'He's no more French, than a bag of sprouts.' But Mr Albert is charming to Aunt Kit and asks her if she might have tea with him one day, so she can tell him of her wonderful work at the hospital.

'Please don't,' cries Millie when he's gone.

'Why ever not?'

'I don't think he's a very nice man. You might not be safe.'

Aunt Kit is looking at her strangely, as if she is concerned she's not well. 'Don't worry, Millie. If I have tea with Mr Albert it will be in a very public place.'

'He'll ask you questions and make notes in his little book.'

'Will he indeed?' Aunt Kit is thoughtful. 'Please don't worry, Millie. But thanks for the warning.'

Millie thinks that tonight's been very exciting. When she'd arrived at their home, Aunt Kit had said she needed to see Martha for a minute. Joe was now in the hospital where she worked, and was well enough for Martha to visit.

Martha had come in to see them. 'Great news, Flo,' she'd said. 'Joe's nearly home.'

Aunt Kit said that they needed to remember that he was still quite weak because he'd lost a lot of blood from the serious wound to his leg. But she agreed the news was good.

They were on the tram going to the theatre when Aunt Kit said to Mumma, 'Joe is such a lovely young man. I hope he makes a good recovery, but not so good that they send him back. And you know, Flo, when he's asleep, Joe keeps saying such a strange thing. *'The Germans knew we were coming. They knew we were coming.'*

Millie had pretended not to listen. She'd stared out of the window. How would the Germans know that Joe was coming to France?

When they arrived at the theatre, Ted told them that there were some trapeze artists in the show, from one of the big American circuses.

'We like circuses, don't we, Millie?' Aunt Kit said. Millie agreed and they'd shared a secret look together.

When the trapeze artistes, The Carlton Brothers, perform their act, Mumma comes up to join them and they look out behind the curtain. A large and very strong frame has been built high above the audience, almost touching the ceiling. From it hang ropes and wooden swings, and two long rope ladders that go right up to the top of the frame.

Mr Albert comes onto the stage and tells the audience that they are in for a death-defying treat. Millie whispers to Aunt Kit to ask her what death-defying means and Aunt Kit says it's very dangerous indeed.

'Ladies and gentlemen, put your hands together for the most marvellous Carlton Brothers.'

With a great role of drums, the four trapeze artistes dressed in white vests and tights with red satin bloomers, wave to the audience, then walk off the stage and climb the two rope ladders.

They take hold of the wooden swings and push themselves through the air over the heads of the audience. As if that wasn't scary enough, the men then do somersaults, flying between the swings. Millie can't believe her eyes. Mumma says that when she first met Papa, he'd been in a troupe just like this one.

Aunt Kit says, 'Oh, my!'

The people in the audience are leaning back, with their faces looking up at the exciting things going on above them. They let out great cries and duck down when one of the troupe pretends to miss his grip and looks like he is going to fall, before, at the very last minute, catching hold of the legs of one of the others.

The theatre erupts with noise, there are whistles and shouts of

'Bravo'. Everyone is clapping and the audience is on its feet. The Carlton Brothers return to the stage for a final bow and Ted drops the heavy red curtain for the interval.

'Blimey, they're good.' Ted says as he joins them. 'If they stay for a few days, we'll be full every show. 'Ere your old man used to do this stuff, didn't 'e? That one pretending to fall got them going?'

They all agree and Mumma and Aunt Kit go on chatting as Ted begins to shift the scenery and bring the props for the jugglers and the magician.

Millie needs to go to the toilet. She jumps down off the basket. She whispers in her aunt's ear. 'I'm going to the toilet, do you need to come?'

'No, thank you.' Aunt Kit is smiling. 'But do you need me to come with you?'

'Oh, no. I know my way, won't be long.'

She skips around the passage at the back of the stage heading for the ten stairs that will take her down to the lavatory. There's usually a queue. As she passes Mr Albert's office she hears shouting. The door has bobbly glass which means you can see the light, but not what is happening inside.

Fascinated Millie peers through the fuzzy glass. She can see the shapes of two men either side of large desk.

'Don't you hoodwink me, you old goat. You've had your money, now you need to come up with the information. Real information, not just your lists.'

'I told you how many men had signed up, how many were training and which regiment. I've done what you asked – don't you double-cross me.'

'You're in no position to issue threats. We know all about you, Albert. One false move, and you're finished.'

Someone comes along the corridor and Millie bends down to pretend to do something to her shoe. They say 'Hi, Millie,' and walk away. Millie knows that there is often shouting in Mr. Albert's office. People get sacked from the show and he's not nice to them, so shouting isn't strange. But this is different. She stands now at the side of the door so she can't be seen by the two men, and listens.

'I've done as you asked.'

'It's not enough.'

'I've given you the information you asked for, now go away.'

'Oh no, that's not good enough. We need more.'

'What more? I've tried the stations and they're crawling with military police.'

'The stations are covered. Get yourself in with one of those canaries. Find out what weapons they're making in that armaments factory of theirs.'

Millie knows they make shells and bombs at the armaments factory and it's very secret. She's sure, now, that Mr Albert is a spy.

He's shouting again, 'Don't be ridiculous. How would I go out with a working girl? And they're none of them too pretty.'

'You're problem, mate. But don't try to pull the wool over my eyes again. Otherwise, you'll need to watch where you walk. Lots of accidents on these busy roads.'

Millie can hear movement in the office and she runs back along the passage, bending to fiddle with her boot again. Mr. Albert's door opens. It's the man with the bowler hat. He strides out and almost knocks her over. He's wearing his brown striped suit. Millie sees that the legs of his trousers are quite tight and he has shiny black shoes with dark socks. He smells funny, like he hasn't washed, but has covered himself in scent instead, sweaty and sweet all at once.

There's a twittering and giggling as the chorus girls trip along towards her. They tickle Millie as they go past.

'Lav's free, Mill,' one shouts back to her. 'Be quick or you'll miss the start.'

Millie runs along and down the stairs. As she heads back to the stage, she can see Mr Albert sitting at his desk with his head in his hands.

'Well, Flo. 'Yer goin' to 'ave trouble followin' that,' Ted is saying.

'Tell me about it!' Mumma says.

Millie's out of breath. 'You'll be just great, Mumma. You always are.'

'What a lovely niece, you are,' Aunt Kit says and gives her a hug.

And Mumma is great. She sings all the old favourites, and when she sings *Mollie Malone* in her very Irish accent, everyone joins in.

And because everyone else is singing Millie stands on the basket next to Aunt Kit and sings as loud and as well as she can, copying the way that Mumma moves her arms to encourage everyone to join her.

'My goodness, Flo,' Aunt Kit says later. 'Young Millie's going to follow in your footsteps. She's a wonderful singer and has a real presence about her.'

And Millie feels very proud.

Daisy is Ill

As Millie and Mumma climb the stairs to their room, Martha comes out to meet them. 'Flo, I'm worried about Daisy. She's fast asleep, but she's burning up.'

Mumma tells Millie to put a kettle on. 'Then get a bowl and a jug of cold water please. Also towels and some of Daisy's old napkins.'

Millie is carrying the jug with cold water when Mumma carries Daisy through, Martha is following.

'Well done, Millie. Now lay a towel down on the rug and we'll get Daisy undressed.' Daisy lies like a doll without her clothes. Her curly hair is around her face, but her cheeks are bright red. Her skin is hot and dry.

'Millie, pour the cold water into the bowl and then top it up with the kettle. It must feel normal to the touch, not too hot and not too cold.'

'Martha, can you open the window for me and jam the door open too, please. Perhaps we'll be able to get a draft through. It's stifling tonight.'

Millie dips her fingers in the water. It feels a bit warm so she adds some more cold water.

Mumma comes over to test the water. 'Perfect. Well done, my darling. Now pass me those napkins.' Mumma carries the bowl across to Daisy.

Mumma and Martha each kneel either side of Daisy. Then they each take a napkin, put it in the water and squeeze most of the water out. Then they wipe Daisy's skin all over, but don't dry her.

Mumma says, 'Hopefully, this way we'll bring her temperature down. Millie, we might need some more water, can you organise that for us do you think? And we need some cooled boiled water for her to drink too.'

To Martha she says, 'She was very grumpy earlier this week. I thought then she might be coming down with something. Sorry that you had to cope with it.' Martha tells her not to be silly.

Millie's pleased they're friends again. She loves Martha and its nice having someone so kind to look after them when Mumma isn't there. Millie wonders when Joe will be home.

After a while, Mumma sits back on her heels. 'I think she's cooler. What do you think, Martha?'

Martha agrees. 'The redness in Daisy's cheeks is lighter and she's nowhere near as hot. I can't believe she hasn't woken up through all of this.'

'No, when Daisy's asleep, there's no waking her. She can sleep with me tonight.'

As they lift Daisy to put her in Mumma's bed, she begins to wake. She whimpers a little, opens her eyes, and gives Mumma and Martha a great big smile, then curls in a ball and goes back to sleep.

'Millie, time you were in bed. Thank you for your help.'

'You're a great nurse's aide. You could be a VAD just like your aunt. Flo, call me if you need help during the night.' Mumma and Martha hug.

After Martha has gone, Mumma says, 'Let's hope we won't have to call the doctor.' Millie knows you only call the doctor in the worst emergency because you have to pay him for his services.

'Aunt Kit would help, Mumma.'

'I know, Millie. And I would ask her if I needed to, but I'm hoping it's not anything more serious than a summer cold. Now off to bed, young lady, and don't forget to go to the toilet and wash your hands.'

Millie wonders why something called a cold would make you so hot. Martha had said that Daisy had been burning up.

When she comes back into the room, Mumma is hanging the damp towels on the airer above the range. 'What an exciting day, Millie. But look at the time, it's after midnight. You can have a lie-in in the morning.'

Mumma comes to tuck Millie into bed. 'God bless. Sleep well,' and kisses Millie on the forehead.

'What are canaries?' Millie asks.

Mumma looks as if she might cry and her voice cracks as she says, 'Millie, let's talk about this tomorrow. I've had just about enough tonight.'

Interlude 4

Daisy being ill has frightened Millie. Her little sister was so hot, her skin burning when Millie touched her. No wonder Mumma had been upset and now, lying in bed, Millie feels tears prickling her eyes. She curls up and hugs her pillow. There's something lumpy underneath it. She'd forgotten all about the little acrobat. She'd hidden him away again after she and Daisy had last played with the circus.

She waits until she hears the creak as Mumma gets into bed, and waits a little longer still until everywhere is quiet. Then, she brings the little acrobat to her lips and kisses him on the top of his head and, in her quietest whisper, she says, 'Take my love to Papa!'

She's in the market square of a little town. It's very crowded, lots of stalls and, what seems like, hundreds of people. Around her are very old buildings. She's seen buildings like this in England, old pubs and sometimes posh houses, but she's never seen so many together. Some have stone walls and others have coloured walls, yellow, cream or pink, and she can see the wooden struts that make the frame of the building.

The stalls are selling all kinds of food, and in cages, there are ducks and chickens, and rabbits. There is a cheese stall that's very smelly, like old socks, and a bread stall with lovely round golden loaves and long sticks of bread too. It smells delicious and Millie remembers she hasn't had anything to eat for hours. Her tummy rumbles.

A woman is sitting by a small table and she's milking a goat. People are giving her jugs and she fills them with the frothy white milk. On the table are small rounds covered in grey as though they've been rolled in ashes and others are wrapped in green nettle leaves. Millie goes closer. Are these cheese?

A man, at another table, has a large jar in front of him and it's full of dark, knobbly, round balls. When he takes one out there is a strong earthy smell. She watches as people smell the balls, nod enthusiastically, and then give him lots of money. He has a large metal box on his lap. He opens it with a key and puts the money in. He must be very rich.

The vegetable stall is full of strange things. Round, pale green spiky things like thistles with a sign that Millie tries to spell out Art-i-chaut, and large dark purple things with a thin skin and a sign saying Au-ber-gine. And beans, long red ones, and green ones too. And a basket of small white beans which look like they have a little black eye. There are huge tomatoes and thin onions and red lettuce. And there are cherries and peaches. Millie's mouth begins to water. She'd like to reach out and take a cherry, but doesn't have any money. She pulls her cotton nightdress around her.

This is very different to the markets at home, much louder, and people are speaking in a funny way. French, perhaps. Just like when Papa said, 'Je suis le petit acrobat.' They wear different clothes, leather, and wood clogs. And there are soldiers too, but they have a dark blue uniform and flat caps. *Not the same blue as the injured soldiers at home.*

But the children look just the same as children at home, though their skin might be a little darker. The sun's out here and much warmer here than at home. She looks at her feet. She's barefooted, like the children, but the cobbles she's standing on are warm and smooth. For a moment she enjoys the warmth of the stones on her toes. It's only when she walks on stones that are in direct sunshine that it isn't nice. These are too hot and it seems like the soles of her feet are burning. Hopping up and down, she heads for the shade again and now she's more careful where she walks.

At the end of the market square, Millie notices the top of a great big blue tent. As she walks towards it, she realises that although it looks big against the market stalls, it isn't huge. It's circular, with a blue top and decorated with a large yellow star right at the point. And the canvas walls are red.

There's a poster close to the entrance of the tent with a picture of a roaring lion which says

'Circus Suisse.

Bergerac

Ce soir 20.00'

Millie spells out the word Ber-ger-ac. It's been written onto the poster in big letters.

Behind the tent are a couple of old gypsy caravans in red and yellow with curved white roofs. Millie is going over to have a look inside when she's distracted by the smell of horses, and walking back towards the market, she finds a pen made out of some iron gates and the market railings.

Tied in the pen is a Shetland pony, a larger white horse and an animal Millie thinks is a camel. She sits down on a kerb and looks at it. The animal has a long neck and a small head, but its coat is white, not yellow like a camel's and it doesn't have a hump. Each animal has a bail of straw and a bucket of water.

In the warm sun, a man is working in his shirt sleeves. It's Papa. He walks over to the little Shetland pony. She's white with patches of brown and as he approaches her ears twitch and she snorts at him. She fidgets, but as he works the brush over her legs, he talks gently to her in French. Millie is surprised she understands what he's saying.

'Bonne fille, Paulette. You are a beautiful horse. Ca va, Paulette, ma petite.'

She's a stocky little horse. He bends to polish her hooves. 'Allez Paulette. Lift your foot. Come on, help me here!'

'Bon. Maintenant, where are your ribbons?' He goes over to a bag hanging on the market railings and finds brightly coloured ribbons which he fixes to Paulette's bridle.

A man walks out of a bar on the corner of the square. He's carrying two glasses of beer on a tray. He hands one to Papa.

'Hey Francois, she looks a picture that girl of yours.' And Millie wonders if they've seen her.

'That she does. She's in good form.' They're talking about the pony. 'Are you bringing your family to the show tonight, Marcel, or will they be keeping the bar open for you?'

'But, of course. When the circus is in Bergerac, everything shuts down. Even the war cannot stop the circus!'

They laugh together. Papa clearly likes Marcel, who seems to be a good friend. Perhaps Papa has to be a friend to everyone in this secret job he has. That way he can go to the bars and cafes and listen as people talk about the war. And people do talk about the war, all the time. In England too. At school they are told often to be careful – Loose Talk Costs Lives. She thinks for a moment of Mr Albert and wishes she could ask Papa what she should do.

Marcel is sitting near Millie, drinking his beer in the sunshine.

Papa says, 'The market has gone on a long time today. It usually closes at lunchtime.'

'Yes, it's because you're here. People are coming in from all over to get some cheer and the market traders never miss a trick. Why close when there's money to be made?'

Papa moves on to groom the white mare. He calls her Eloise. He goes to her head and talks to her, telling her he's going to make her beautiful for Jacqueline. 'Two beautiful girls. The crowds will come to see only the two of you.' He gives her a carrot and the mare snuffles his hand.

He starts to groom Eloise with a flat brush working it over the horse's body.

'You seem a happy man,' Marcel says. 'Content in your work.'

'I'm as happy as any man who has to travel from his Canton, and I miss the mountains. But yes, it's a good life.'

'My boys are looking forward to seeing you do your acrobatics. You've built quite a reputation along the Dordogne for your speed and agility. Quite fearless, they tell me. Not something I'd thought of before, a Swiss, being good at tumbling and somersaults.'

Millie notices that although Papa is still grooming Eloise, he is watching Marcel carefully, as if working him out.

'Oh, Marcel. You know how it is. It's the same the world over. I was a small boy at school. If I hadn't had a special talent, the bullies would have made my life a misery. Some kids are the jokers in the pack, some are good at sport. What about you?'

'Oh, I was the joker. Kept me out of trouble. Well, my friend, I'd best be getting back.' He gets up. 'Bring me that glass when you've finished with the llama. He's my favourite. Fancy calling a llama, Spitz. But I'll look forward to seeing the girl who dances on the horses back, she's a rare talent.'

Of course, it's a llama, from Peru. She wonders if this one had come to the circus on a boat and been flown through the air like the horses she'd seen.

'Bye, Marcel. Thanks for the beer.'

Around them the market traders are packing up. Lorries and wagons drawn by horses have arrived to take away the produce that is left. Papa moves on to the llama, walking around him with great care. But Spitz is happily munching away on some straw, and let's Papa groom his long mane and polish the short hair on his haunches.

A thin, short lady with blonde hair comes out. She's dressed in a long cotton skirt and has a white blouse.

'Francois, I've made us something to eat before the show. Just some pasta, but it should fill us up.'

'Thanks, Jacqueline. I'll be right there.'

Papa finishes his task and gives each animal a pat on their bottoms as he leaves. He stops close by where Millie is sitting and looks directly at her, but doesn't seem to notice her. He's deep in thought and turns to look once more at the bar. Papa must be careful. No-one likes a spy.

She has been holding the little lead acrobat and senses that it is time to go home. She kisses the top of his head. 'Keep Papa safe,' she says.

Millie is back in her bed. It's very quiet and still dark. She can hear Daisy snoring gently and Mumma's bed creaks.

Mumma calls gently, 'Are you OK, Millie?'

'Yes, thanks. How's Daisy?'

'Much cooler. Sleep well.'

Millie lies for a few minutes thinking about Papa. Is *Bergerac* in the Dordogne? The Captain on the ship had said Papa was going to the Dordogne. She'll try and find out where that is in France. It's very warm there, hotter than summer. She's falling asleep, when she wonders why she hadn't stayed to see the show.

Act 4

Auntie Annie

The next morning is Saturday and after breakfast Mumma has said Millie can go out with her friends.

'You were such a kind girl last night. So helpful with Daisy. It's a lovely day. Go and have some fun.'

Millie is up and dressed and jumping down the steps before you could say 'Jack Robinson'. As she runs to find Mary, Millie wonders who Jack Robinson is and why everything to do with him is so quick.

Mary's coming back from the market with shopping. 'Can you play today?' Millie asks her.

'Let me get this back to me Mam and see what she says.' The girls walk together, each holding a loop of the cotton shopping bag. 'Careful, Millie. There's eggs in there and me Mam'll be mardy if they're broken and then we won't be going anywhere.'

'Hello, Mrs Jarvis,' Millie says. 'Can your Mary come out to play, please?'

Mary's Mam is ironing just as Mumma does at home, the heavy iron warming on the range, a large white sheet on the big kitchen table. 'Did you get me list?' Mary nods. 'Well, I should think so then, but wouldn't you like a biscuit and a drink before you go?'

Mrs Jarvis puts two small cups of milk and a small plate with broken biscuits at the end of the table and the girls clamber up on the bench.

'How's your Daisy, Millie?' she asks. 'I heard she was proper poorly last night, poor little bairn.'

'She's better, thank you. Mumma says she's cooler today. We didn't need to call the doctor.'

'Well, that's good news, lass.' She turns back to her ironing.

Millie says, 'Mrs Jarvis, what's a canary, please? Isn't Mary's aunt one?'

'Yes, that's right, Millie. She went to work at the armaments factory when some of her friends joined up. She said she wanted to do something for the war too. She's doing that all right, it's no picnic working there.'

'I don't know why she would be called a canary.'

'Oh, that's easy,' said Mary. 'It's 'cos the stuff she works with's turned her skin yellow…like a canary.'

Millie munches on a bit of biscuit. 'Do all the ladies and men who work at the factory have yellow skin?'

Mrs Jarvis smiles. 'No, not all – just the ones that work with the TNT, putting it into the shells, like my sister, Annie. They have to pour it in from great big metal jugs, and however careful they are, it seems to get right inside of them. One poor girl had a yellow bairn only the other day.'

'Is their work secret?' Millie asked.

'I should say. Though everyone knows what they make at that armaments place.'

As they run out together, Millie asks Mary if they might go by the factory. 'I don't think I've ever been.'

'Come on then. It's nearly 12 and they'll be coming out. We might see Auntie Annie. They look a bit strange, you won't be scared will you?'

Millie thumps her playfully on the arm and they both run off through the park.

As they get to the factory gate, they hear the loud siren which announces the end of the morning shift. 'I'm puffed,' Mary says.

'Me, too.' And they laugh as they each bend over to catch their breath. A man in uniform comes forward to heave open the two huge iron gates. He nods at Mary.

'Morning lass. Who's this then?'

'My friend, Millie.'

'I see. As long as *you* know her, then that's alright. Can't be too careful.'

'They don't like people hovering round the factory. You're only allowed here if you're related like, meeting someone. Otherwise they move you on.'

Millie looks around. There are a few people waiting, some young men, older women with children, and a couple of soldiers in uniform. But not many. There's a low rumbling noise which turns into a roar as, what seems like, hundreds of people come from several doors and gather on the factory forecourt. As they pass the man at the gate they shout, 'Bye, Jim.'

Mary jumps up and down to catch a glimpse of her auntie, and then drags Millie back across the road. 'It'll be easier to see her here.' There are men in overalls with their flat caps and big boots. And women, young and old, wearing large brown aprons that wrap right around them and on their heads they wear brown mop caps to cover their hair. And the skin of many of the women is yellowy-orange. You notice it more when they're together. One waves her yellow hand high above her head. She's young and pretty. 'Hello, me duck,' she shouts.

'Hello, Auntie Annie. This is Millie. She's my friend. She's never been here before, so I brought her to see you'

'Pleased to meet you, Millie'. She holds out her yellow hand. Millie hadn't bargained for this, but shakes Auntie Annie's hand and as she does, Aunt Annie gives her a little curtsey. Laughing, she says, 'You'll do. Now I must be off. Tell yer Mam I'll pop in for me tea tonight. Bye.' Annie runs off to catch up with a couple of other girls.

Millie looks at her own hand. She gives it a sniff. It's got a funny smell, like matches after they've gone out. The factory workers have nearly all gone now and Jim is closing the gates. They make a huge clanking sound when they shut together. He waves to Mary and Millie.

They turn to walk back through the park and Millie sees the large shape of Mr Albert barring the way at the park gates. 'What are you doing here, Millie?' he asks.

Millie wonders what to tell him. But Mary says, 'She's with me. Come on, Mill. We've time to play on the swings.'

'Who's he?' Mary asks her. They both turn to walk backwards so they can see Mr Albert.

'He's in charge of the theatre where Mumma works. But he's up to no good and he's got to meet a canary.'

'Jim'll sort him out. You ain't allowed to loiter by the arms factory.'

'Doesn't your aunt mind being yellow?'

'She did at first, but they give her lots to eat. Me Mam says she's put on weight since she's been there.'

As they turn to run home, Millie smells her hand again and wipes it down her skirt. She wonders if it will turn yellow too, but, Mary's is a pink, normal colour and she sees Auntie Annie lots, so perhaps it'll be alright.

Joe Comes Home

As Millie runs into the large courtyard of her tenement, she finds noise and commotion. At the foot of the steps a motor ambulance has drawn up and two men in uniform are helping Joe out of the back and into a wheelchair. Martha is there, and Aunt Kit.

Joe's left leg is out straight and bandaged right the way along. He's holding onto one of the ambulance men as he's lowered into the wheelchair. Joe's face is very white, his eyes seem to have sunk into his head, and he's thinner.

'You mustn't put any weight on it, mate,' one of the ambulance men says, nodding towards Joe's leg, 'or you'll open up that wound again.' They push Joe towards the stairway.

The other's scratching his head, looking at the stairs. 'Two flights, you say. Not sure how we'll manage that. I should think once you're up there, you won't be going out again.'

But Aunt Kit takes command. 'For goodness sake, he's come all the way from France in much worse condition, I'm sure we'll manage the stairs.' She steps back to take a look.

'Joe, do you think you could sit on the stairs and hoist yourself up? We'll support your wounded leg.'

After what seems forever, Joe arrives at the top of the first flight. With an ambulance man either side of him, he stands upright.

Families have come out onto the landing to see what's going on. Gladys, Bert's wife, is there too. There's a complaint from upstairs, and Gladys, calls back, 'Be quiet, you old fool. Young Joe's home and that's much more important than your sleep.' She's smiling, 'Ee, how are you, me duck? You look right poorly. Let's find this lad a chair.'

Someone brings a wooden chair out onto the landing. Joe smiles as he sits down.

Aunt Kit says, 'Millie, run and get me a small towel please. That's been hard work for Joe.' She's looking at Joe's bandaged leg as Millie runs off. She finds the towel, and grabs Joe a drink of water too using a metal cup she finds by the sink. Mumma always says water's good if you're not feeling well.

When Millie gets back, there's a little crowd around Joe. He smiles at her, 'Hello, Mill. How you doing?' and the neighbours move back so she can get in.

Martha says, 'You need to take this one back with you, Kit. Uses her head, young Millie. She's a real VAD.'

By the time they reach their own landing, Joe is very tired. Martha goes for a chair this time. To the ambulance men, Aunt Kit says, 'Thanks for your help.' And they say 'Good luck, mate!' But Joe only seems able to smile and nod to them.

'Leave the wheelchair at the doorway, please,' Aunt Kit calls to their backs as they walk downstairs and they wave to show they've heard her.

'Will it be safe there?' Millie asks.

'I should think so,' Martha says. 'Not even the rough necks that live here would dare to play with a wheelchair for a wounded hero.'

Mumma has joined them. 'Hello, Joe. It's good to see you, my dear.'

'How's Daisy? Ma said she's been really ill.'

'She's getting there. She's a tough little mite.' They smile at each other and Mumma puts a hand on Joe's shoulder.

Millie says, 'Can I help Martha look after Joe? She says I'd make a great VAD.'

'No, Millie. You're too young.'

'It'd be great if Millie could do some fetching and carrying for me, Flo,' Martha says. 'Would that be alright?'

Mumma smiles, 'Of course,' she says.

Daisy comes peeking around the door in her nightdress. 'Me hungry,' says Daisy.

'Me too,' says Joe.

'I've got steak and kidney and dumplings on the range,' Martha tells him.

'My favourite,' Joe says.

Aunt Kit says, 'I'd better head off, Martha. I'm on duty at 4pm and have a couple of things to do before I start my shift.'

'Thank you for your help, my dear. Will you not stay for something to eat?'

'Thank you, Martha. That is so kind of you, but I really must be on my way.'

Joe's getting flustered. He catches hold of Aunt Kit's hand. 'I need the toilet. Can you help me before you go?'

Aunt Kit bends down to Joe and, although Millie listens hard, she can't hear what they are saying.

'How can you go to the toilet if you need help to do things?' Millie asks.

Mumma says, 'Millie!' in her cross voice.

'Good question, Mill,' Joe says.

Aunt Kit is laughing. 'Out of the mouths of babes and sucklings,' she says. 'Martha, perhaps you have an empty milk bottle Joe could use?'

A deep voice from the stairs says, 'Now, ladies, about your business. This is man's work. Joe and me will sort this out.'

It's Bert, walking down the stairs in his night shirt, long johns and boots. As he steps onto the landing, he stands to attention and salutes Joe. Joe salutes back.

'What are you doing now?' Gladys asks him.

'Helping this young warrior. Now make way!' Bert says.

'You're in good hands,' says Aunt Kit, 'Eat well and you'll heal and get stronger quickly. I'll be back tomorrow to see how you're getting on.'

Mumma says, 'It's going to be strange, Joe, for a little while. But it's so good to have you home.' And to Millie and Daisy she says, 'Come on, girls. In we go. Let's have some lunch. Tell me what you did with your friends, Millie.'

And Millie tells her about Mary's Auntie Annie and the armaments factory and how she knows now what a canary is.

Helping Martha

Millie has been so busy helping Martha and Mumma that she can't remember what she's done over the last few days, or when she did it. Only school has been the normal thing in her life. Here she's been able to play with her friends and forget about grumpy Joe and 'Millie, do this' and 'Millie, do that.' She was so tired on Friday she didn't go with Mumma to the theatre. And every night when she's put her head on her pillow, she's fallen fast asleep.

Walking into the market on another trip to do some shopping for Martha, she wonders when it will end. There have been rows too. There are always rows on the other landings, but not on theirs. The other day when Martha and Bert were trying to get Joe to use his crutches, he'd thrown them across the landing and shouted at his mother.

Bert had said, 'No need for that, lad. Yer Mam's only trying to help.'

And Joe had shouted, 'What do you know, you fat old fool? What do you know, staying cushy here and sending young men into hell?'

Millie thought there'd be trouble, but Bert had only said, 'I know, lad. I might be too old for this one, but I know. And yer Mam is only trying to help, so pack it in.'

Mumma had said Bert had gone up in her estimation that day. 'Of course, he knows. The poor blighter was in the Boer War, and that was no picnic.'

'Joe says his leg is very painful,' Millie says.

'Well, so it might be, but Kit says it's healing and he should get himself moving, not go throwing crutches at his mother and old men.'

Martha had taken a cake for Bert and Gladys to say sorry. She'd popped in later to apologise for the rumpus and told Mumma that Gladys had shown her Bert's medals.

'Sit down, my dear. You look all in,' Mumma says helping her to the chair by the range. As Mumma is making her a cup of tea, Martha's face crumples and she starts to cry.

'Take Daisy out to play please, Millie,' Mumma says.

The job Millie likes best of all is helping Martha mangle the washing. She's never been allowed to help with it before. Mumma had said it was too dangerous, but when Martha asked if Millie might help her, Mumma had finally agreed.

'Keep your fingers well away from the rollers, Millie,' she'd said. 'You will need every one of them and the hospitals are too busy to have to worry about cutting off the squashed fingers of careless children.'

Martha had gasped. 'Flo, I daren't take the child to help now.'

But Millie had laughed. 'She just wants me to be careful,' she said.

'Well, make sure you are,' Martha said. 'Mangles can be tricky. Perhaps if you are strong enough to turn the handle, I can push the washing through.'

And she had been strong enough. Martha had been careful not to put too much through at once and Millie had turned the handle which turned the rollers. She had watched as the water trickled out of the washing into the tin bath below. Lots of it. The bigger things like sheets had to be put through twice. The first time the water splurged out, and the second time it trickled out. She learned that you mustn't be too quick or the rollers don't have time to work. But at the end, the sheets are almost dry, and if you're clever folding them, almost flat.

'Can I help you too, Mumma,' Millie had asked later.

'Why not?' Mumma had said. 'You're growing up, Millie. Getting taller and wiser. Won't Papa be surprised when he gets home?'

Millie and Daisy Put on a Concert

The next time Aunt Kit comes to tea, she brings news that Joe's leg is healing well. 'He should use it more, but he seems to do nothing but sit in his chair. He's putting on weight and looks much better. He's moving more easily too.'

'He can go to the toilet on his own,' Millie tells her.

'Yes, thank you, young lady,' Mumma says. 'I think that's more information than we need.'

'Millie's right, Flo. He's strong enough now to get to the toilet. His balance is good. But otherwise Martha can't make him budge from his chair. I think he's bored. And if we can't lift him out of it, I fear for his mental state. Martha's got enough to worry about without that. The only good thing is that he's keeping his grandad occupied playing endless games of draughts and dominoes. But it's not what a fit young man should be doing.'

Millie has an idea and, after Aunt Kit has gone, asks if she might take Daisy for a walk to the park. Even though they've had tea, the sun is still shining and it's warm out.

'Bring the dolls,' she tells Daisy. She picks up her slate and chalk.

At the park they rehearse their show again. 'We're going to do a show for Joe to cheer him up,' Millie tells Daisy. 'You've got to be very good and dance well. When I tell you to stop, you must stop. No tantrums.'

They practise the songs and dances, and Millie writes a programme onto the slate.

> *The Misses Elliot*
>
> *will perform –*
>
> *Daisy Belle*
>
> *Molly Malone*
>
> *Tipperary*

About an hour later, they knock on Martha's door. 'Daisy and I have a special surprise for Joe,' Millie says.

Together they organise some space and three chairs for Martha, Joe and Grandad. Martha and Grandad look very interested. Joe doesn't seem bothered at all. Millie props the slate on the dresser and explains that the Misses Elliot will be performing a show and that this is the programme.

Millie sings *Daisy, Daisy, give me your answer do…* as Daisy dances around with a big smile on her face. Grandad and Martha sway in time with the music, but Joe just looks bored. Millie notices that he seems more interested in a newspaper than he does the concert. As they finish the number and take a bow, Joe doesn't clap, but Grandad stands up and claps loudly, shouting 'More, More.'

'Sit down,' Martha says. 'Then they can do their next number.'

Mumma has come across to see what all the noise is, and Bert and Gladys are standing with her at the door.

Millie announces that the next song is *Molly Malone*.

'My favourite,' says Grandad.

Millie works hard to stay in tune. Daisy dances in her funny way. As she reaches the chorus, everyone joins in. Everyone, except Joe. At the end of the song after Molly's ghost has wheeled her barrow through streets broad and narrow, Grandad is on his feet joining in the last long chorus. The audience at the door is laughing as well as singing and, Millie can see that even Joe is smiling just a little watching his Grandad.

There is a great round of applause and Millie and Daisy take their bow. 'For our final number,' Millie says, 'We will sing *It's a Long Way to Tipperary*.' This song has a long verse and Millie has told Daisy that they will hold hands and march on the spot as she sings it. So she gives a cough and works hard to remember the words.

At the chorus, which is much easier, Millie and Daisy begin to march around in a circle. Millie had wanted to lead the march herself, but she can't keep her eye on what Daisy is doing, so lets her sister lead instead. Daisy is very good and even salutes as she marches. Millie salutes too and Grandad leaps up from his chair and marches behind the girls.

Half way through the chorus, Millie becomes aware of another noise, and she stops to listen. Loud, heavy sobs and wails of pain. She sees that Joe is crying, his face crumpled. Almost immediately Martha is by his side and is holding him close to her.

Daisy has started to cry and Mumma gathers her up taking her back across the landing. Millie gathers up her slate and follows them. But Grandad is cross and comes to the door. 'No,' he shouts, 'Hey, come back, you haven't finished the song.'

Bert comes to their door. 'Flo, any chance the youngsters can finish the show here, do you think? We have an old soldier who was really enjoying it.'

Mumma doesn't look very pleased. Gladys appears with her arm around Grandad. 'The girls were brilliant, Flo. He loved the singing. Do let them finish.'

'Please, Mumma,' Millie says.

'What about Joe?' Mumma asks.

'Oh, I think the show's been good for Joe too,' says Bert. 'He won't think so now, but tomorrow it'll be different.'

'Come on old timer,' Gladys says. 'Let's see if these girls will sing for you again.'

And so with Mumma's help, they arrange another stage area. Millie and Daisy sing and dance their concert all over again and Grandad sings with them, every song. Millie can see that Mumma is very pleased. When they get to *Tipperary* again, although they sing it much more quietly than before, they all march in a line behind Daisy.

'I'll sing one now,' says Mumma and leads Grandad to the chair by the fire. She sits on the floor beside him. Millie, Bert and Gladys sit at the table and Daisy sits on Gladys's lap. Mumma sings very gently. It's a love song Mumma sings at the theatre, *Let Me Call You Sweetheart.*

When Mumma sings the song a second time, Millie gets down from the table and goes to stand by her. She holds Mumma's arm and gently hums the tune as Mumma sings. By the time they've finished, Grandad is fast asleep. He's snoring quietly.

'Well, haven't we been the luckiest people in the whole world this evening, Glad?' Bert says. 'You have two chips off the old block 'ere, Flo. Delightful.'

'Well done, girls,' says Gladys.

Mumma gives them a hug. 'How about some supper and then I think it's time you two were in bed.'

Martha pops in later. 'How's Joe?' Mumma asks.

'Sleeping like a baby, now. Thank goodness. That song seemed to unlock something for him. Who'd've thought it? Where's Grandad?'

'The same,' says Mumma, nodding at the chair by the fire. 'Leave him there, Martha. No need to disturb him. I'll bring him home when he wakes.'

'Millie and Daisy, thank you, my dears. What kind and talented girls you are.'

When Mumma comes to tuck them in that night, Millie asks her about Joe. 'Why was he crying? Is it because he's missing his friends or was his leg hurting?'

'It's a lot of things. It's difficult for him being here when he knows his friends are fighting in France. His leg wound will leave him with a limp and he won't be going back.'

Millie thinks Joe's silly. He's safe here, even if he does have a bad leg. Not like Johnny's dad who isn't coming home. They know that now. A letter arrived to say he'd died. Johnny had been allowed to bring some of his things, medals and his hat, to school to show the class.

Mumma says, 'Your show really was really good, you know. Papa would have been so proud, just as I was. And you've got me thinking.'

'What about?' says Millie.

'Early days,' Mumma says. 'Let's wait and see.'

Adults are always doing that. Let's wait and see what?

Interlude 5

Daisy has fallen fast asleep almost as soon as her head hits the pillow. It's been such an exciting day. When they'd climbed into bed, Joe's Grandad was still in the chair by the fire. Mumma's busy doing some ironing and singing gently as she works at the table. Millie wishes Papa could have seen the show. Perhaps when he's home again they can do it for him. She puts her hand under her pillow and takes out the little acrobat. When she holds the little figure, it feels as if Papa is close by. Without thinking, she kisses the top of his head and says, 'Take my love to Papa, Acrobat!'

Millie finds herself in a large field. A little way off is the circus tent and she can see Eloise, the white horse roaming freely in a large roped off area under a tree. That's better than the tiny stall in the market. The horse has green grass to eat here.

Although it's a sunny day, there's the smell of wood smoke, like a bonfire.

She hears voices coming from one of the red and yellow caravans and wanders up to have a look. She climbs onto the little ladder that leads to the door, like a stable door, half open at the top, half closed at the bottom. After three steps she can see into the caravan itself.

It's tiny. Much smaller than the room they live in at home. It can't be much bigger than their two sleeping cupboards put together. In front of her are two long benches with blankets, either side of a long table. At the back of the caravan is a stove with a strange looking pot. It's tall and made of metal, light blue, and steam is gently puffing from a long spout. Above this are cupboards and shelves packed full of dishes and pans, and pretty painted boxes, blue with pink roses.

Papa is sitting on one side of the table. 'I must take some of these posters to the next town,' he says.

Jacqueline is sitting at the other side of the table. 'You're always busy. But we did well here in Villebois this week, didn't we?'

Papa is putting piles of coins and notes into a metal box on the table in front of him. 'Yes, the takings are up,' he says. 'They come to see you and Eloise. Two beautiful girls.'

He's laughing. Jacqueline hits him playfully with a tea towel as she gets up and goes to the back of the caravan. 'Always flattering to deceive,' she says.

Mumma says that too? Flattering means you say nice things about people and deceive means to trick them. Millie laughs. Yes, it's a good way to describe what Papa does. Jacqueline comes back with two white bowls. She has her cloth around the handle of the funny shaped pot and pours a brown liquid into the bowls. It's hot and Millie can smell it, reminding her of Christmas. They have tea at home most of the time, but at Christmas her parents have real coffee, made in a jug.

Jacqueline picks up the bowl in both hands and sips her coffee, but Papa, who is writing something in a book, picks up the coffee bowl by the rim with one hand, blows on it and takes a gulp. When he puts it down again he's got a big brown ring of coffee around his mouth. It makes him look like a clown. Jacqueline takes a hankie out of her pocket and wipes his face. He laughs, catching her hand to kiss it.

Hey, that's not right. He shouldn't be kissing anyone, but us. Millie stamps her foot angrily. How dare he? He should save his kisses for Mumma. But Papa is talking again. 'Well, my beautiful Jacqueline, I have to love you and leave you. These posters won't stick themselves up. Old Reynard should be in for his money in an hour or so. Keep it locked away until then. Here are the keys.'

'One of these days, you'll say he looks like a fox to his face and then where will you be?'

'Out on me ear, I shouldn't wonder. OK. Mon-sieur Rey-nault. Must be nice sleeping in a soft hotel bed whilst the rest of us have to do with a hard bench and horsehair mattress. My back aches this morning.'

Papa's at the door and Millie jumps down off the ladder. 'Zac and Bernard are doing the animals today. A few more days and we're out of here.' He waves to Jacqueline and heads off. He has a large roll of papers under his arm. Millie follows. She would've liked to have taken his hand, but is frightened she might give herself away. He heads round the back of the caravan and picks up a large bucket with some squidgy paste and a large flat paint brush. Then he walks to the gate at the side of the field which leads to a rough road.

They walk down to a crossroads and Millie can see a signpost which says 'Brantôme.'

After a couple of minutes, she hears the clatter of hooves and a horse drawn cart comes into view. There are hay ricks in the back. Papa waves.

'Bonjour, Monsieur. Allez au Brantôme?'

'Oui, Monsieur'.

'Can you take some company?'

The man thinks about this. 'Oui, je vous en prie.'

Papa climbs up to sit beside the man. Millie only just has time to climb up onto the hay. She didn't think she'd make it, she'd stood on her long nightdress and got stuck. But as the horse starts to move, she lands softly on the hay. And now they're off, lolloping along the road.

Papa and the man are chatting away about the harvest. 'The hay's in now. It's sunflowers this week, and the maize a couple of weeks later.'

Lying there is the warm sun, looking up at the sky, Millie listens to Papa and the farmer and the clip clopping of the horse's hoofs. The sun's warm and she drifts asleep.

She's woken as the cart stops and Papa jumps down. His boots clump as he lands on the road. Millie realises that it's too high to jump. 'Don't move, horse,' she says quietly and it blows through its nose at her, as if sensing she's there. Holding onto the side of the cart, she steps onto the top of the big cartwheel, then onto the spokes, and now she can jump the rest of the way. Thankfully Papa and the farmer are still talking. The farmer is pointing to another road.

'Merci, Monsieur,' Papa says.

The farmer waves, 'A bientot.' He jollies the reins and the horse clops off again.

Papa and Millie walk into a big white and grey town. Millie can see a river running through the centre and over it are lots of bridges. As they go along, Papa takes one of the large pieces of paper from under his arm and sticks it on a wall or a notice board. It's the same circus poster as before, but this one says Brantôme, instead of Bergerac.

Millie would like to help. It looks fun. Papa takes the brush from the bucket and paints a thick layer of paste onto the wall about the size of a *poster. Then he unwraps a poster and lays it onto the wall. Then with more paste, he paints over the poster. Job done. And on they go.*

As he works, Millie looks around and can see why the town is white and grey. The walls of the buildings are painted white, and in the sunshine, they're shining. The roofs are grey and the buildings have large grey stones usually at the corners, left bare. All the bridges, and there are so many of them, are grey too.

They pass a few people as they walk along the little streets and alleys, but no one pays them much attention. It's only when a group of children clatter around a corner and almost bump into Papa that excitement grows. All the children wear clogs and carry books under their arm. Perhaps they've been to school. They point to the poster, before running off chirruping like sparrows. But one child, a boy, comes back and looks right at Millie, puts out a hand as if to touch her. She stands as still as she can. His friends call him and he runs off.

On the other side of the river is a huge white and grey church, with other large white and grey buildings alongside. Behind and above is a high cliff with trees on the top. Monks, dressed in long black habits with big hoods, walk below the cliff and through pretty gardens which surround the buildings. They must be very hot, it's a warm day.

As Papa and Millie walk over a bridge towards the church, a large wooden mill wheel is turning, forced around by the strength of the river. She'd like to stop and have a proper look, but Papa is heading towards a large wooden door in the side of a building next to the church.   He still has one poster left and Millie can see that there's another smaller piece of paper rolled inside.

There's a funny pull thing by the door and Papa gives it a tug. A bell tinkles somewhere in the building. After a moment or two, the big wooden door opens with a loud creak, and a monk in black stands at the door. He has a tanned face and brown hair cut like a circle around his head, with a bald patch in the middle. Around his neck is a chain with a heavy wooden cross and tucked into the belt around his middle is a set of large wooden beads, like a necklace.

His eyes are dark, but he smiles at Papa and makes the sign of a cross above his head.

'Welcome, my son,' he says. Millie thinks this is a funny thing to say. Papa can't be his son, he's not French.

Papa says, 'I have the poster for the abbey. I have carried it far.'

And the monk says, 'The journey is long to reach an Abbot.'

Are they mad? Millie looks at them both and wonders if she hasn't understood. It doesn't make any sense. But the monk opens the door wide and Papa and Millie go in. She finds herself in a huge hallway.

'I cannot stay more than a moment or two, Father,' Papa is saying. 'I don't think I was followed, but you never know. And I don't want to put you and the order at any risk.'

'We are used to risk.' the monk is saying. 'Do you have anything to report?'

And Papa takes the final poster and the paper he's been carrying inside. This is my report in code, of course. I have included everything I have found out. There is much enemy activity in this area of France. The German agents operate in the cafés and bars, gathering and sharing intelligence.'

'Sadly, you are right, Francois. Have you heard them talking about information coming from England?'

'Yes. There's information about the number of men who have signed up. And much interest about the armaments factories in London and the Midlands. This isn't unusual, of course. This you would expect. We need the same information about the Germans.'

'Have you been able to find out the source of this information?'

'No, but worryingly, there are mutterings about the music hall. Though for the life of me, I can't see how that would work.'

'That is your background, my son.'

'Yes, and my wife still works in the local music hall. I do hope she and the family are safe.'

Millie can't believe what she's hearing.

'You must miss them.'

'Father, they mean everything in the world to me. I miss them terribly.' Tears roll down Millie's cheeks when she hears this. Papa doesn't love Jacqueline. Only them. She wipes her eyes on the sleeve of her nightdress and sniffs.

'You're a good man, Francois. And a brave one. Very few could have maintained their cover in the way you have done.'

'I'm luckier than those poor souls at the front.'

The monk is speaking again. 'We all want to restrict each other's ability to amass weapons. Information will help the Germans to pinpoint and bomb the armaments factories with their dreadful Zeppelins.'

'We leave Villebois in the next day or so and expect to be here in time for the weekend. Our stay in Brantôme is short and then I must leave. My cover won't last for much longer.'

'No, my son. You must take care. You will give Arnaud your last report. You know where to meet him?' Papa nods. 'Then, God speed.'

They move towards the big door again.

'Thank you, Father.'

'Travel safely, my son.' And the monk blesses Papa again as they walk out.

Millie had expected to arrive back in the sunshine, but she finds herself in bed, still clutching the little acrobat. She's frightened. She kisses the top of the little acrobat's head and whispers,

'Keep Papa safe.'

She wonders if Mumma will have realised she's been away. She can hear voices.

'Come on, Grandad.' It's Martha. 'Time to go home. Thank you so much, Flo. I've got so much done this evening and having time with Joe on his own was very special.'

'We've had a good evening, haven't we? How is Joe?'

'Still sleeping. Thank the girls in the morning for me. I expect they're both fast asleep.'

'Not a peep from either of them.'

'Night, Flo.'

'Night, my dear. Night, Grandad.'

Millie hears Grandad say, 'See you in the morning.' And then the door closes.

Millie would like to get up and talk to Mumma, but isn't sure what to say. She knows too that the concert has caused Mumma extra work, it wasn't meant to. Funny how things don't work out the way you plan them.

Mumma puts her head into their little bed cupboard and is surprised to see Millie awake. She bends to kiss her and Millie puts her arms around Mumma's neck and holds on tight, breathing her soapy smell.

'Do you think Papa will be safe?'

Mumma looks at her. 'I do hope so, Millie.' But Millie can see she's worried. Giving Millie another hug, Mumma says, 'Good night, my clever darling.'

Millie thinks about the monk who blessed Papa and how Papa

said that Mumma and Daisy and Millie meant everything in the world to him. He has to be brave and clever, to pretend to be someone he isn't so he could find out information. To help us win the war. She is still frightened for him, but very proud too. She thinks that it must be the same for everyone who has someone at war. As she closes her eyes, she says a prayer in her head for Papa. 'Please keep him safe.'

Act 5
Ted Gets a White Feather

Mary says, 'You know that bloke that was hanging around the factory?'

'Mr Albert?'

Mary nods.

'What about him?'

'Well, he's taking Auntie Annie out tomorrow. They'll probably go to the cinema.'

They are walking home through the park.

'She mustn't trust him, Mary. He's not a nice man. He'll ask her questions and try to find out information.'

'Will he? How do you know that?'

Millie's just about to tell Mary that she'd overheard Mr Albert being told to take out a canary and get information from her, but something tells her that she needs to be careful. Who'd take any notice of what she had to say, anyway. Just like Papa, she needs to watch and listen, take it all in.

'Race you to the big tree,' Mary calls before Millie really knows what's happening, but she chases after Mary and they both bang into the tree together. 'Dead heat!'

Sitting under the tree to catch their breath, Mary says that

Millie's a good runner. 'I thought I'd win, but you caught me up, uphill too.'

'I like this tree,' Millie tells her. 'It's a great place for a picnic. You can see right out over the park. We saw the White Feather Brigade give a feather to a man who wasn't in uniform.'

'Me mam hates them. They gave a feather to her young brother and he went to war. He's a tall lad, but he's only sixteen. They shouldn't have done it. Mam says he's no more than a boy. He's in France now.'

'Why do they take boys?'

'S'pose they need all the soldiers they can get. So they're not choosy.'

'Joe's home now,' Millie tells her. 'He won't fight again. He can't walk and he's not eighteen yet. Mumma thinks it's her fault, 'cos she was singing at the theatre and he signed up there and then.'

'That's boys for you. No sense. Why not wait until they're the right age?'

'There's my friend, Ted. He works at the theatre.' Millie stands to wave, but at the same time she sees the White Feather Brigade. They've seen him too.

'I must warn Ted, Mary. Help me shout.'

The girls stand up and shout, '*Ted. Run, Ted. Run, Ted.*'

'They mustn't give him a feather. He tried to join the army, but they wouldn't have him. He's got asthma.'

'What's asthma?'

'It means he can't breathe. *Leave him alone.*' They set off down the hill, rushing towards Ted and the woman walking up to him.

'*Leave him alone. Leave him alone.*'

'Why don't you mind your own business,' the woman says. 'Clear off, you ragamuffin.'

'You mustn't, he isn't well.'

'He looks well enough to me. Go away, you nasty little tyke.'

'Millie,' Mary says. 'Look.'

One of the women is handing Ted a white feather, but he won't take it. He's trying to explain. She's not listening, so he ducks out of the way as she tries to put it in his jacket pocket. But at the same time, another woman has come behind Ted and has caught hold of him by his shoulders. Now the first woman stuffs the feather up his nose.

'You horrible old woman,' Mille says and kicks the woman's ankles.

'Riff, raff,' the woman says, hitting Millie over the head with her handbag.

Mary is trying to pull Millie away. Ted has taken the feather out of his nose, but has started to cough. He bobs down on the ground, wheezing badly.

'What the hell is going on here?' a huge booming voice says. Millie looks and sees Martha bearing down on them.

'Oh Martha,' she says. 'These horrid women have given Ted a feather and he's got asthma and now he can't breathe.'

Martha seems to take in the scene all at once.

'You mean old bags,' she says to the women. 'Get yourselves out of my sight or I won't be accountable for my actions. Pompous, self-righteous busybodies.'

'We're only doing what's right. Every man should be fighting for his country. Those that don't are cowards.'

'And you have sons and husbands fighting, do you?'

'That's not the point.'

'Oh, I think it absolutely is the point. My boy went at seventeen because of ignorant people like you. And now he may never walk again. Get out of my sight, you old hags.' Now Martha starts to lay about them with her shopping bags.

Like hens, the women cluck and fuss, but leave and a great cheer goes up from a bunch of people who've stopped to look.

'Millie, don't let me ever catch you kicking a lady again,' Martha says pointing her finger menacingly. 'And who's this?'

'It's my friend, Mary.'

'Well, she looks terrified, poor mite.'

'I'm worried about Ted,' Mary says.

And Ted is in trouble. He's wheezing badly, gulping for air.

A man comes up with a cup of water. 'This might help,' he says.

'He tried to join the army,' Millie says, 'but they wouldn't have him.'

'Well, you can see why,' the man says. 'Those women are a curse. My neighbour joined up last week. He's forty-five years old and has five kids. His wife can't cope, even when he's there. She'll never cope now he's in France.'

Millie is sitting with Ted now and holding his hand. 'It'll be alright,' he says, 'if I can sit for a while and lean forward like.'

The park-keeper arrives with a wheelbarrow. 'Ere,' he says. 'I don't mind giving you a lift. 'Where's 'ome?'

Martha says, 'Ted can come home with us. I'd rather see he's properly recovered before he goes home.'

'I'll be alright,' Ted says between coughs.

'Stop arguing. Flo will never forgive me if I don't bring you back.'

'She won't. It's true,' Millie says.

So off they go. Ted in the wheelbarrow pushed by the park-keeper, Mary and Millie either side of him, each with a hand on his back, helping him to sit upright. Martha is leading the way talking to the man who brought the water. Ted is still wheezing, but he seems to be breathing a little more easily now.

Joe and Ted

When they get home, Millie runs up the two flights of stairs to Mumma. 'Mumma, quickly. It's Ted.'

'Where've you been girl? Have you seen the time? I've been worried sick.'

'It's Ted, Mumma. They put a white feather up his nose and brought his asthma on. Martha shooed them away and the park-keeper brought him home.'

'What rubbish are you talking, Millie? This better not be a fancy tale to divert my attention, young lady.'

'It's not, I promise. He can't breathe and Martha brought him here for you to see him.'

'Oh, for goodness sake. You bring Daisy. Let's see if this might help.' And she bustles around picking up a bowl, the kettle, a towel and, from the high cupboard, a small jar of camphor crystals. She puts them all on a big wooden tray and they head downstairs.

'Mumma's good with emergencies,' Millie tells Daisy as she shuts the door. 'Now, take care. And don't be scared. It's only Ted.'

'What's all the fuss about and where's me Mam?' Joe is standing at the doorway supported by his crutches.

'I can't help you, Joe. I've got to look after Daisy.'

'Where's your Mam going with that stuff?'

'It's our friend, Ted. He's got asthma and the park-keeper's just brought him here in a wheel-barrow,' she calls as she heads downstairs with Daisy.

'Course, he has,' says Joe. But Millie knows he doesn't have any idea what she's talking about.

When they arrive at the bottom of the stairs, Ted is sitting in Joe's wheelchair leaning forward over the bowl with a towel over his head. He's taking deep breaths. He's still coughing, but the wheezing is much better.

Millie lifts the corner of the towel to take a look at him and the thick menthol steam feels warm against her face. She takes a deep breath herself and then starts to cough from the fumes.

'Will you get out of there,' Mumma says.

A small crowd has gathered. Mainly mothers with their barefooted children.

'Should we fetch a doctor?' one asks.

'You going to pay?' another says.

But Martha has a better idea. 'How about a nice cup of tea? What about you, Ted?' Ted nods his head underneath his towel.

The man from the park and the park-keeper both like the idea of tea too. And Mumma agrees.

Suddenly there's a huge clatter as two crutches slide at their feet, and bobbing down the stairs on his bottom, his leg out straight in front of him, comes Joe.

'Blimey, that was hard work. What's going on? Did you say you were making tea, Mam?'

Millie runs up to him and gives him a hug. 'You're clever,' she says. 'Fancy getting down all that way on your own. You're very hot. Are you tired?'

'I'll say, but the fresh air's good.' He takes a deep breath. ''Ere, that's my wheelchair!'

'Well,' Martha says. 'We didn't ever think you'd want to use it. By the way, it's nice to see you out and about, so to speak.' Millie looks at Martha, she's smiling, but her eyes are hard.

'She's like my Mam,' Mary says. 'Being sar-ca-stic. Saying something nice, but meaning something else.'

Millie says, 'It is. It's lovely that you're out and about, Joe. This is my friend Mary. She was with me when Ted was attacked.'

'What do you mean, attacked?'

'He got white-feathered,' said Mary, 'but Millie kicked the ankles of one of the women.'

'Did she, by Jove? Quite a firebrand.' Mary and Millie give Joe his crutches and with the help from the men from the park, he manages to stand himself up straight. There is a great round of applause. And 'Hello, Joe' and 'Good to see you, Joe.' Joe smiles and tries to wave.

There's quite a party whilst they drink their tea. Gladys arrives with some freshly baked biscuits and even Bert comes down to say Hello before heading back inside. He's still in his nightshirt and the girls giggle. Gladys tells him not to be such an old exhibitionist.

'Wait till Aunt Kit sees you,' Millie tells Joe. 'She'll be really surprised.'

'If I can't get back up, she certainly will.'

'You can go back up the way you did when you came home.

Mary and I'll carry your crutches.'

'I've landed in a world with women who nag. You should try it
Nelly-Know-All.'

The men from the park have finished their tea and are starting
to say good-bye. 'Come and see us, Ted, Joe.' Millie thinks Joe
will grumble, but he surprises her by saying, 'Thanks. I'd like
that.' Ted takes the towel away from his head and says thank
you.

'You look better,' Mumma tells him. 'Do you think we should
get you home?'

'I'd like that,' Ted says.

'Right. Joe, can I borrow your wheelchair to get Ted home?
It's not far but I don't think he'll cope with a tram.'

Ted is breathing more easily now and sitting up strongly. 'I
think I can walk, Flo.'

Joe says, 'You know, mate, I think you should accept the ride.
Be on the safe side.'

Ted says, 'Thanks, Joe.'

'My pleasure, mate. Gawd, you wouldn't have lasted five
minutes over there. They was right not to take you.'

Ted is looking sad. 'When I'm breathing properly, I'm strong. I
can shift scenery and stuff like that. Could I come over and
push you, do you think? Perhaps we could go to the park, or
the pub.'

'Yeah, good idea. I'd rather a bloke pushed me out, than me
Mam.'

'Well, thank you very much,' Martha says, but Millie can see
she's very happy.

'Come on, Mary. You can walk with me,' Mumma says. 'Millie, keep an eye on Daisy, please. Get yourselves some bread and jam and get ready for bed. If you need anything, call Martha.'

'Do you mind if I sit on the stairs for a bit, Mam,' Joe asks. 'I'll come up when Flo gets back.'

Martha puts a hand on his shoulder and kisses the top of his head.

'Shout if you need me,' she says.

Flowers from Ted

Millie's been busy. She's given the circus a good clean. She washed the little figures in soap and water and dried them on a cloth, before standing them on the window sill to finish drying in the sunshine. They look very smart lined up in the light. Mumma has given her a little polish for the wooden hoops and she's given them a shine too. Now she's tipping the little bits of dust and fluff out of the boxes, so they're ready to receive the clean circus. Daisy is playing with the dolls. Mumma has been doing the washing and Millie is waiting for her to call and help with the mangle.

Aunt Kit had come round for her tea yesterday. And she was very pleased to hear their news about Joe. She'd popped in to see him afterwards and they'd heard shrieks of laughter. 'Isn't that a great sound, now,' Mumma had said.

There's a knock on the door. Millie finds Ted carrying two big bunches of flowers.

'They're pretty,' Millie says. Ted just smiles.

He gives a bunch of flowers to Mumma.

'Thank you, Ted. You're looking much better.'

'I wanted to say thank you for helping me.'

'That's kind, Ted. Millie, go and fill a glass for these. They'll brighten the table nicely.'

When she comes back, Ted says, 'And these are for you and Mary, Millie. Not much, but I wanted to thank both of you, as well.' He gives her a bag of sweets. They're sherbet lemons, her favourite. You suck them and they're quite sweet and hard, but then the soft acidy lemon sherbet comes through, and you have to pucker up your mouth.

'Yes, they are. Thanks Ted. I'll take them to share with Mary later. Who's the other bunch for?'

'Martha.'

Later when Millie is helping Mumma mangle the water out of the clothes, she can hear Ted talking to Joe.

'I expect they're making plans for an outing,' Millie says.

'I do hope so. It'll be so good when Joe gets out and about. He'll feel better and make life easier for Martha.'

But Millie has plans for Joe and Ted herself.

Mille Has News

A few days later, Millie is able to see Joe and Ted on their own. Mumma has taken Daisy shopping and to see some of her music hall friends. Martha is out too. Grandad is sleeping in his chair.

'There isn't much time,' she tells them when Ted has opened the door to her knock. 'I have to tell you this. It's really important and I might not be able to tell you everything.'

'Sounds intriguing,' says Joe.

'It's really serious,' says Millie. 'But I need grown-up help. Grown-ups that won't laugh at me.'

'Can't guarantee that, Mill. Depends how daft it is.'

'There's something that's not right. Not right, right here under our noses.'

'Go on,' Ted says. 'Don't leave us in suspense.'

'Ted, have you noticed Mr Albert with a notebook and how he's always noting things in it with a pencil?'

'Yes, but he's in charge of a big theatre and has lots to remember. He needs a notebook, I should think.'

Joe says, 'It's what he takes notes about that's important. That's what's worrying you, Millie, isn't it.'

'Yes, I noticed it first the night you joined up, Joe. He was at the back of the theatre taking notes then.'

'Was he, by jingo?'

'Yes, and then I've seen him watching the new soldiers when they're training on the park.'

'Still, making notes?'

Millie nods. Joe rubs his chin. 'If I thought that snake had done for us, I'd kill him with my bare hands. The whole battalion said that it felt like they knew we was coming.'

'I can't think old Albert is a spy,' said Ted. 'He's not bright enough.'

'He doesn't do it on his own,' Millie said. 'There's a man like a weasel, who wears a brown stripy suit and a bowler hat, and he shouts a lot at Mr Albert.'

'Yes, I've seen him,' Ted says. 'He's old Albert's friend. A Mr Fisher. I thought he was from Head Office.'

'Perhaps, you've got the wrong end of the stick, Mill,' says Joe.

Millie had known it wouldn't be easy. She'd thought a lot about what she would do if they laughed at her.

'But, Joe. This man gives Mr Albert lots of paper money for pages out of his notebook. I saw that myself. And he's told Mr Albert that his information isn't good enough. That he needs to go out with a canary and find out about the factory. And he's going out with Mary's Auntie Annie. She's a canary.'

'He's just an old man who likes the company of young women,' Ted says. 'He's not the only lonely old man who wants to spend time with them.'

'He's more than that, Ted. There's something not nice about

him.'

'Well, there's a whole load of difference between not being nice and being a spy,' Ted says. 'I heard that now your mam's retiring he's thinking of showing films at the theatre. They're the big new thing. He's even said I could be the projectionist, if I keep my nose clean.'

'What's a projectionist?'

'I'd show the films.'

'We're getting off the point,' Joe says. 'Millie, you say you think this Mr Albert is a spy and that he's gathering information for a Mr Fisher?

'Yes.' She puts her hand into her pinafore pocket and brings out the piece of paper from Mr Albert's book. The page she'd used to copy down what she saw there. 'Look at this.' She hands it to Joe.

He reads it out loud.

28th May 1916

10 x 8 = 80 men

Drill Sergeant from North Notts Artillery (France)

Rifles

'When did you get this?' Ted asks.

'That day I came to bring him a message from Mumma. I saw his coat over his chair in his office and thought I'd try to see what was written in his book. It was in a silky pocket on the inside of his coat. There were lots of pages like it and pages torn out. But the telephone rang and you came to answer it and I had to hide under his desk. It was very scary. '

'You're making this up,' Ted says. 'I'd 'ave seen you if you was in the office.'

'It was someone wanting to talk to Mr Albert. You told the other person that Mr Albert couldn't be disturbed because he was au-dit-ion-ing and to ring back again in the afternoon. You said you'd take a message.'

'It was that Mr Fisher,' Ted says, scratching his head. 'Blimey, Millie you sure know how to take the wind out of a bloke's sails.'

Joe is laughing out loud.

Millie is cross. 'Don't laugh, it's not funny. Don't laugh at me.' She thinks she might cry. This is horrid.

Joe smiles. 'I'm not laughing at you, Mill. I'm just amazed. What a girl, you are. You took a rare chance, Millie. Not sure I could be that brave.'

'Oh,' Millie says. 'It didn't feel very brave. I just needed to know. It didn't seem right. And they say at school *Lose talk, costs lives.*'

'They're right. And you think he's trying to get information out of Mary's Auntie Annie now?'

Millie nods.

'Why've you told us?' Joe asks.

'Because no-one will believe me if I go to the police, because I can't prove anything. And anyway who'd ever believe a girl? I thought if you knew, you could confirm what I'm saying.'

'Well, we can't, can we? 'Cos, we ain't seen it,' Ted says.

'No, you haven't.' Millie has to agree.

'But, if we did see it,' Joe says. 'Then we could tell them.' He has a strange look on his face, sort of excited. 'What 'arm could it do. It'd be our mission, Ted. If you're still up to taking me out.' Ted isn't looking so sure.

'Leave it with us, Mill,' Joe says. 'We've got some planning to do. Have you told Kit?'

Millie shakes her head. 'Not yet.'

'Well done, Mill. Always thought you were a bright little spark. But you're brighter than that. Tell Kit, Millie. She's right trustworthy. Can I keep this paper?'

Millie nods, but now it's done, Millie feels empty. It had been her who had spotted Mr Albert and found out about the weasely Mr Fisher and now Joe's in charge. That doesn't seem fair somehow.

Later she overhears, Martha talking to Mumma. 'I've no idea what's got into Joe. He's full of energy and planning outings with Ted. He's talking about going to the theatre on Friday. I can't keep up with him.'

Aunt Kit Comes to Tea

It's Saturday and Aunt Kit's coming to tea. Millie had decided to tell her what she's found out, but Aunt Kit has been so busy at the hospital, they haven't seen much of her lately.

Joe and Ted have been occupied going out together. It's good to see Joe out and about. Ted helps him down the stairs and then pushes him along to the park. They're out now. With long summer evenings, they stay out forever.

Millie's got to find a way of speaking to Aunt Kit on her own. It's important. She doesn't want to tell Mumma. Now that her time at the theatre is coming to an end, Mumma seems unhappy, restless. Millie wonders if it's because they haven't heard from Papa for such a long time.

'Mumma, please may I take Aunt Kit out for a walk, whilst you put Daisy to bed? Then when I get back I'll help you with the washing up and then go to bed myself.'

'It's not up to me, Millie. Aunt Kit might be tired and want to rest. She's been so busy at the hospital.'

'Oh,' Millie says. 'So, may I go and wait for her at the tram stop and walk back with her?'

'Oh, for goodness sake, Millie. Stop mithering. But if you do all your jobs, you can go to meet Aunt Kit.'

Millie had worked hard. She's done the shopping, helped Mumma wash up after she'd baked cakes for tea. She's taken Daisy to the park and laid the table. She looks at the clock.

She's got 5 minutes to run to the tram stop. She grabs her hat and runs off down the stairs.

Mumma calls, 'Go steady, child.'

Millie worries that she's late and has missed Aunt Kit, but there's a queue waiting at the stop and a lady tells her that the tram hasn't arrived yet.

Soon, the box shape of the tram comes into view. Millie always thinks it looks like an insect with its red and cream paint, dark windows like eyes, and two antennae fixed to the power lines above it. It makes a whirring noise like a large fly. There's the tinging of a bell and the tram comes to a stop beside her. A few people get off and finally Aunt Kit steps down. She waves when she sees Millie waiting for her.

'Hello,' she says, bending to give Millie a hug. 'This is a lovely surprise.' She holds Millie out in front of her and says, 'My dear child, whatever is the matter?'

Millie can't contain herself. 'Oh, Aunt Kit. It's all wrong. Joe and Ted are going to catch Mr Albert being a spy. But it was me that found out first and now I have nothing to do.' Despite wanting to be grown-up, she's close to tears.

'Oh, my goodness,' says Aunt Kit. 'This sounds serious. Let's sit on that bench for a moment.' She has her arm round Millie. 'Tell me all about it.'

'Mumma will be cross if we're late for tea.'

'Is it going to take the rest of the day to tell me then?'

Millie shakes her head.

'Well, then how about starting at the beginning.'

'You mustn't tell Mumma. I think she's worried about Papa and I don't want to worry her with this.'

'I'm not promising that, Millie. If Flo needs to know, we must tell her. But tell me about it first and then we can decide.'

So Millie explains all that she has found out and how she has told Joe and Ted and how they are out spy-catching without her. 'I told them and now they've left me behind.'

'Well, there may be a good reason for that, Millie. Spy catching is very dangerous work.'

'But, it's still not fair. I did all the work and now I've been left out.'

Aunt Kit is silent for a moment. 'Well, I agree,' she says finally. 'It must seem a little unfair.'

'It seems a lot unfair,' says Millie.

Aunt Kit laughs, 'Yes, I think you might have a point.'

'I found out about Mr Albert, and Mr Fisher. I found out about the canary and Auntie Annie too.'

'You did very well. You have been very observant, my dear. And clever, to put it all together, like a big jigsaw puzzle. Oh, Papa would be so proud of you.'

They sit together for a few minutes watching the road. As people pass them, they nod politely and say good afternoon. Gentlemen lift their hats to Aunt Kit.

Aunt Kit says, 'I think it's because you feel you have nothing to do now. Is that right?'

Millie nods.

'Right, first thing to remember, young Millie, is that you have done something the rest of us have been trying to do for weeks. You just don't know how clever you are?'

'What have I done?' Millie isn't so sure she's done anything so great.

'You have given Joe something to get his teeth into. You have given him back his reason for living. He now has a *raison d'etre.*'

'What's a *raising dater?*'

Aunt Kit laugh's 'A *raison d'etre.* It's French. In its purest sense it means a reason to be. But really it means you have given him back his purpose in life and that's very precious.'

'Is that good?'

'It's more than good. It's just brilliant. You have given him back his energy, his motivation to get better. You are very clever.'

Millie's still not sure. 'Well, I'm still stuck here on my own, and Joe and Ted are out spy-catching.'

'Will you trust me, Millie?'

Millie nods.

'Thank you for telling me. It means we are very good friends. Keep watching, Millie. Keep finding out. They can't do it all. Please don't take any more chances. Will you promise me that?'

Millie nods.

Aunt Kit says, 'But this needs some coordination and I'm not convinced Joe or Ted can do that.'

Millie starts to feel a bit better. That's what had worried her. That they would go off and see and do things, and not tell her. Not join it up.

'Time, we headed home for tea. It's gone 3,' Aunt Kit says.

'Oh, Mumma's going to be very cross.'

'The tram was late, and that was true,' Aunt Kit said.

An Idea for a Concert

Mumma had been a bit grumpy, when they'd got home, but Aunt Kit has soon cheered her up.

Mumma is pouring the tea, when Aunt Kit says, 'Flo, you know you told me about the girls' concert?'

'Yes. Although it ended in tears, Joe seemed to perk up after it.'

'Grandad sang songs,' says Daisy, and she shows them how he'd sung. 'He said, Come back, come back!' Everyone laughs, she looks so comical standing on the bench and pretending to be an old man.

'Sit down, Daisy,' Mumma says. 'Before you fall off.' But she's laughing too.

'It was a lovely evening. They did a lot of good in their small way.'

'Well, I mentioned it to the Matron. As a VAD I'm not really supposed to talk to someone as important as her, but she and my mother were at school together. I've had tea with her a couple of times in her sitting room.'

'Oh yes?' Mumma is smiling, but Aunt Kit hasn't noticed. Millie has seen that when Aunt Kit is saying something about how posh she is, Mumma has this smile that is not an unkind or cross smile, just an amused smile.

Millie is just trying to remember what a cross smile might look like when Aunt Kit says, 'Yes. And Matron thought that it might be a wonderful idea if the wounded soldiers, particularly the ones who are well on the way to recovery, could have a concert to cheer them up.'

'But there must be people who can play a piano and organise a sing-song.'

'Oh, there are. But that's not the same as having music hall stars come to perform to them. And maybe music hall stars' children!'

'Oh, please can we do it, Mumma. Do a concert. Say yes, say yes. Please, say yes.'

'We'll see,' Mumma says.

'O-wa,' Millie says. 'That means it won't happen.'

'It's quite a commitment, Flo. I understand that. But it seems such a shame to hide all this talent away when you could be bringing such joy to men who've fought for their country.'

'Alright,' Mumma says. 'You're as bad as your brother. Don't go flattering to deceive me, Miss Elliot. I'm a past master at recognising baloney.'

Millie gasps, but Aunt Kit and Mumma are laughing.

'Give me a week or so to think about this, Kit. In principle, the idea's a good one. I need to talk to Joe too before I say yes.'

'Thank you. You come back to me when you're ready.'

'Frank and I have always said we wouldn't allow the children to be misused. They need their education and local friends.'

'I understand, Flo. It was only to offer concerts locally and although Millie might be old enough, Daisy is still only tiny. You might not want her involved at all.'

Millie looks across at Daisy, but she's busy feeding cake crumbs to the dolls and hasn't heard. Phew.

As Aunt Kit leaves, she says, 'Millie, walk down stairs with me, will you?'

When they get to the bottom, Aunt Kit is severe. 'Don't press your mother about the concert. It's her decision and she doesn't need you nagging her. Do you understand?'

Millie nods.

'I need to hear you say yes, Millie.'

Millie has never seen Aunt Kit so stern. 'Yes, Aunt Kit.'

'Good. Now, leave the other business with me, please. If you see anything that concerns you. Keep it in your mind just as you have up to now. You can tell me when we meet again.'

Aunt Kit bends down and gives Millie a kiss and Millie puts her arms around her neck and gives her a hug.

'It'll all work out, Millie. You'll see,' she calls as she heads off towards the tram stop.

Missing Papa

'Golly, it's close this evening,' Mumma says. 'I shouldn't be at all surprised if there's not a storm brewing.' She walks over to the window and looks out at the sky. Millie and Daisy have been playing with the circus. Now the figures are cleaner they seem to sparkle. Aunt Kit had been impressed when they'd shown her. Daisy has taken charge of all the animals and with Mumma had collected small cardboard boxes which they'd painted and cut bars into the side. Here the animals wait before they go into the ring to perform. Millie can almost hear the lions roaring.

She's in charge of the ring master and all the clowns and acrobats. And the white horse. Mumma had said she was very creative when she'd told her that the horse's name was Eloise and the dancer was Jacqueline. Not for the first time, Millie felt like she'd let Mumma down by keeping an important secret from her. She isn't creative, just mean, and it doesn't make her feel happy. She brushes away her tears.

She feels herself gently raised from the floor and put on Mumma's lap. 'Hey, what's up with you, young lady?' Mumma says.

Millie sobs. She wants to tell Mumma about seeing Papa and everything he's doing. She wants to tell her how unhappy she is now that Joe and Ted are chasing spies. But she says what's really in her heart. 'I miss Papa so much. Will he ever come home again?'

And for the first time, since he'd been away, Mumma whispers, 'I don't know, Millie. Every day I pray he will. But with no news, how can I say? No news is so hard to bear.'

'So why do people say, no news is good news?'

'It's quite comforting in a funny way. Because you don't know, you can still hope.'

'But it might not be good news.'

'No, it might not. And all we can do is to keep praying and keep hoping.'

Mumma had been right. That evening there'd been one of those summer storms that light up the sky. Millie knows that once the storm has passed the air will be cooler. She quite likes storms. Not if she's out in them of course, but watching them from a window is fun. She likes the flash, crash, wallop.

Best of all she likes counting between the lightning flash and the thunder clap to work out how many miles away the storm is. Flash. One, two, three. Crash. Three miles. If they come together, the storm is right overhead. Flash, bang, wallop. This one has been overhead for ages now. The biggest flash of lightening streaks across the sky at the same time as a great thunderclap. Daisy is hiding her face on Mumma's lap, but Millie's enjoying the storm. The next time the lightning flashes, she counts one, two. 'Oh, it's moving away. That's not fair.'

'Thank goodness for that,' says Mumma. 'Now look at the time. Bed.'

Interlude 6

Millie and Daisy both wake when there is another crash, bang, wallop. And Daisy starts to cry. 'Don't cry, silly. We're fine here, all snug in our little bed.' But Daisy is sitting up now, yowling.

Mumma arrives in her nightgown. Daisy walks across Millie's tummy to get out of bed. 'Hey, watch out you great elephant,' Millie says.

'If I take Daisy in with me Millie, will you be alright?' Millie thinks about this for a moment. She'd been brave for Daisy, but storms seem worse at night.

'I'll be fine, Mumma.' There's something she wants to do.

As soon as she hears Mumma's cupboard door closing, she takes the little acrobat from under her pillow, says, 'Take my love to Papa, Acrobat,' and kisses the top of his head. She lies there with her eyes tight shut, but nothing happens. She's still in her bed. What's gone wrong? She starts to panic. Has something terrible happened to Papa? She is about to cry out to Mumma, but stops herself. Think, Millie. What did you do? She tries again. This time she kisses the top of the little acrobat's head and, then says, 'Take my love to Papa, Acrobat.'

She's sitting at a table in a bar. Papa is with her. On the table in front of him is a bowl with coffee grounds in the bottom and a square sheet of paper with golden crumbs. He's been writing a letter and sits back in his chair to read it.

Millie gets up and goes to stand behind him.

Somewhere in France, 1915

Dearest, darling girls,

Although you can never receive this letter, I want you to know that I am alright. I hope sincerely that it won't be long before we are together again, my work here is almost done. It has been so hard being away from you all, but then I am not alone in that.

Say hello to Kit for me. I expect she is busy at the hospital.

My love to you all, always,

Frank (Papa)

Papa throws some money onto a little plate on the table, calls, 'Au revoir, Monsieur,' and walks out. Millie can see that he's still in Brantôme. But today, along the river banks, there are market traders setting up their stalls.

She stays close to Papa as ponies pull carts loaded with vegetables, chairs, fruit, cheese.

Papa walks quietly away from the town to the back of the mill. Here he takes out a box of matches and sets fire to the letter he has written. When it's almost burnt up, he drops it into the river. He watches it as it floats downstream. Millie wonders how many letters he has written that he couldn't send. He lights a cigarette and looks back at the town. She senses his tiredness. A man is coming across the bridge. Millie sees that it isn't a straight bridge. It has a right angle, like an elbow, in it so you have turn a corner as you walk across the river.

She's about to go and have a look at the bridge, when she realises that Papa is alert. He's watching the man, but out of the corner of his eye. He takes the cigarette from his mouth and throws the stub into the river.

Papa walks to meet the man as he steps off the bridge. He's been carrying a newspaper under his arm and now he puts it on the wall of the bridge.

'Bonjour, Monsieur. Comment ca va?'

'Ca va, bien, Monsieur. Et vous.'

'Oui, ca va.'

'Le soleil est plus fort, aujourd'hui.'

'Oui, et le tempete passe.'

What is this, Millie wonders. The sun is stronger today and the storm has passed? It's like it was with the monk, saying strange things that make no sense.

Papa and the man chatter about the circus and Brantôme and how busy the French markets are despite the war. The newspaper falls to the ground and Papa puts his foot on it.

Then speaking very quietly, the man says, 'You've done good work, Francois. Thank you. We know now what has been going on. Your information about the new acrobat grenades was the last piece of the jigsaw.

Just a few lose ends to tie up in England. When will you leave?'

'The circus closes here tomorrow and I've told them I have to get back to Switzerland early. My mother is unwell. I'll help them pack up, and then head off.'

The man nods.

'You'll find everything you need. Well, it's time I was off,' says the man more loudly now. 'Don't want to miss the best produce. Bon chance.' They shake hands and the man walks away with a wave.

Papa bends to retrieve the newspaper, looks at the first page and tucks it under his arm. He turns to look across the river and away from the town and, following his gaze, Millie sees the little circus stretched out on a large grassy park.

They walk across the river, turning at the elbow of the bridge to cross to the other bank. Millie can see what she hadn't seen before, that the main river has lots of streams coming into it and the bridges join the patches of land that make up the town.

As they get to the circus, Papa goes up the steps of the red and yellow caravan. Millie can smell wood smoke and coffee. He takes a box out of a cupboard above the stove, unlocks it with a key in his pocket. Now he opens the newspaper, takes a brown envelope which has been tucked in between the folds, and puts this into the box before locking it once more and replacing it into the cupboard. Carefully Papa replaces the key in his pocket.

Then he walks out of the caravan into the big tent. Millie follows running to keep up. They stand watching as Jacqueline practises with Eloise. She looks funny because her tights and tutu have holes in them. On her feet she has a pair of dirty ballet shoes.

She is standing on one leg on the back of Eloise as the horse trots around the ring. Her arms are outstretched and she has her other leg up behind her. Now Millie sees that a man is standing in the middle of the circus ring and has a long rein in his hand. He's guiding the horse.

*'I think she's ready,' Jacqueline says. 'Stay steady, girl. One, two, three.'
And as if she is flying through the air Jacqueline jumps in the air, turns a
somersault and lands back on the horse. She struggles to keep her balance.
Millie gasps. That was even more exciting than the trapeze artistes at the
theatre. She claps and claps. Papa is clapping too and says, 'Bravo, ma
chere. There are very few equestrians who can do that trick. Bravo, ma
petite!'*

*Jacqueline sits down onto the horse's back and brings Eloise to a stop, then
slides off. She runs to Papa and hugs him. Millie feels uncomfortable.
She hates this. But she sees that it is Jacqueline who hugs Papa. He just
lets her hug him, and he has his hand on her back in a friendly way only.*

*'Do you feel confident enough to do that at the performance tonight?' he
asks.*

*'Perhaps. We'll have to wait and see if Eloise is as calm then as she was
just now.'*

'Don't take any risks, will you.'

*'Oh, I'm not the one taking risks,' Jacqueline says as she walks out of the
door, and although Papa laughs, Millie senses her father become tense.
Like he had when he was talking to the man called Marcel. He goes over
to the horse. From his pocket, he takes a small apple and laying it on the
palm of his hand, he gives this to Eloise before stroking her muzzle.*

*'Thanks, Bernard,' he says. 'You did a good job keeping Eloise calm.'
The man smiles.*

Millie is back in bed. Is Papa really coming home? She kisses
the top of the little acrobat's head and says, 'Keep Papa safe.'
The storm has passed and it is cooler. She remembers that
Daisy is in with Mumma and stretching herself out across the
bed, she falls fast asleep.

Act 6
Ted Runs an Errand

Once more, Millie is turning the handle of the mangle for Martha. It has become a regular job for her.

'I don't know what's got into Joe and that lad, Ted,' Martha says. 'They're out all the time. I've told Ted he should sign up to help at the hospital, they need porters and it'd give him a uniform of sorts.'

'Perhaps you should tell Aunt Kit. Perhaps she could sort him out a job.' Martha had liked that idea.

'Come and have a cup of tea and a bun, Millie. You'll need it after all that hard work and Grandad will be pleased to see you.'

Grandad had been pleased to see her and he'd kept Millie busy performing Tipperary and Mollie Malone.

Millie has just said goodbye to Grandad and Martha when Ted comes up the stairs. He's puffing. 'Are you alright?' Millie asks.

He nods. 'Just the girl I want to see,' he says between breaths.

'Why?' Millie asks.

'Never mind, why. Come with me.' He seems very excited.

'Mumma will be expecting me,' Millie says.

Ted bangs on their door. 'Hey, Flo. Can I borrow young Millie here, for a few minutes?'

'Whatever for?'

'Oh, why do women always ask questions? You never take nothing at face value.'

'Cos, we can't trust you lot, one inch.'

'Charming.'

Millie is laughing. Mumma and Ted are always like this. Him complaining about women, her complaining about men.

'Don't take her far,' Mumma says.

'What if I don't want to go?' Millie asks, getting in the swing of it. Mumma's laughing now.

'Gordon Bennet! Please come, Millie. It's ever so important.'

'Gosh, that sounds interesting, Millie. Perhaps you'd better go. But don't keep her out too long.'

Millie grabs her hat and follows Ted down the stairs. 'Where're we going?'

'You'll see.'

News

After a moment or two, Millie realises that they're heading for the park. As they walk along the path Ted waves up the hill in the direction of the old tree and three figures wave back.

'Are we having a picnic?' Millie asks. Although it's late summer, the evenings are still long and warm.

'No,' Ted says. And then he says, 'Do you remember it was here that it all started, Millie?'

'What started?'

'Oh, don't start that again.'

'Well, stop asking such strange questions. Tell me.'

'It all started when I was attacked by the White Feather Brigade and when we get up to the tree you'll find out what's been happening since then.'

She waits as Ted climbs up the hill. It takes a bit of time because he has to stop every so often. But Millie can see the three people under the tree. Just as she'd thought. Joe, Aunt Kit and Mary's, Auntie Annie are sitting on a large checked rug, smiling at her.

'Hello, Millie,' they say when she arrives and Aunt Kit gives her a hug. Joe is sitting with his back to the tree. He's holding Auntie Annie's hand.

'What's going on?' Millie asks.

'Here's our conquering heroine,' says Joe.

Millie's fed up. They all seem to be teasing her. 'If you won't tell me what's going on, then I'm going home,' she says crossly. 'And what started when Ted got his white feather?'

Aunt Kit seems shocked. 'But that's not true, Ted. It started long before you were involved. Millie, my dear, we have some news for you. Come and sit down.'

And then between them they tell Millie what has been happening. Aunt Kit starts, 'You remember, Millie? How you thought that Mr Albert was up to no good?' Millie nods.

'Well, you was right,' Joe says. 'He wasn't.'

Aunt Kit says, 'He was spying on the recruiting teams and the soldiers in training.'

Millie is excited, 'And he had to meet a canary and get information from her.'

'Yes,' says Auntie Annie. 'You told Joe and Ted that, and they came to see me.'

'Annie and I went to school together. We was quite sweet on each other then.'

'They're still quite sweet on each other,' Ted says. And Millie laughs.

'So you didn't go out with Mr Albert, then?'

'Oh, I did,' says Auntie Annie. 'But only in a pretend way.'

Aunt Kit says, 'Because of what you had told us, Millie, we were able to take your concerns to some people in the government who might be interested. One of them was a friend of Papa's, at the Ministry of Information, and between us we set a trap. We couldn't tell you because it was very dangerous. And what you didn't know, you couldn't tell.'

'I wouldn't have told,' Millie says.

'They didn't tell me, neither,' says Ted. 'I was just the poor donkey pushing the wheelchair.'

'Never mind, let's not dwell on anything unpleasant. Suffice it to say, that what happened could only be known by those immediately involved.'

'And that was me,' says Auntie Annie. 'It was me who had to cosy up to Mr Albert.' She shivers. 'And me what was charged with feeding him a line.'

'What does that mean?' Millie asks.

Aunt Kit explains. 'It means Annie had to trick Mr Albert into believing a lie. A very dangerous lie about the ammunitions that were supposed to be being made at the factory.'

Millie still doesn't understand.

'Papa's friend at the Ministry of Information told me that they had thought vital information was getting from England through to France, and then on to Germany. But they didn't know how. It turns out it all came through the music halls.'

Millie understands now. 'From Mr Albert and Mr Fisher.'

'Yes,' says Aunt Kit. 'Mr Fisher was running traitors in music halls up and down the country, but mainly in the towns and cities with armaments factories. Using blackmail to get them to do what he wanted.'

Annie says, 'I had to tell Mr Albert about a new hand grenade we was making, and he told Mr Fisher.'

'Though we've found out, his name should be *Heir Fischer,*' Joe says.

Millie gasps, 'Is he German?'

'No, but he is a traitor, and he was buying information to sell on to the Germans.'

'They're both behind bars now,' says Ted.

'What was the name of the grenade?' Millie asks.

Auntie Annie pats the side of her nose. 'That's secret. I mustn't say the name. And the fewer people who know, the fewer there are who can tell.'

'Is it a real grenade then?' Millie asks.

'Oh no,' says Auntie Annie. 'It's not real. It's just a made-up name. A name that is very unusual, stands out, but might be real.'

Aunt Kit says, 'Because the name is unusual, it can be traced easily. If it's heard of in France, we know the information came from here.'

Millie starts to understand what she's heard on her trips to see Papa. And the acrobat grenade. But she's still not sure. Did she really see him?

Frightened in case she might give herself away, she asks, 'Does this mean you and Auntie Annie are sweethearts, Joe?'

They all laugh. Joe looks sheepishly at Auntie Annie. 'S'pose so,' he says.

'What do you mean? You suppose so. The answer's yes.'

'Time to go,' says Aunt Kit. 'We need to get this young heroine home and it'll turn damp soon.' They start to pack up.

'Does Mumma know about Mr Albert?' Millie asks Aunt Kit as they walk home.

'She may have heard rumours, but it's not common knowledge yet. Has she said anything to you?' Millie shakes her head. Aunt Kit says, 'I'm planning to pop in this evening and tell her myself. I'd like for both of us to tell her.'

Telling Mumma

And they did tell Mumma, sitting at the large wooden table over a cup of tea. Millie and Aunt Kit told about how Millie had helped to catch a spy and break a German spy ring.

Mumma is astonished. 'And you say that the man you went to see about this is a friend of Frank's?'

Aunt Kit says, 'Yes, they were at school together. When I told him about Millie, he roared with laughter.'

'Why did he laugh?' asks Millie. 'Is it funny?'

'Only the connection. That you are his friend's daughter. They have been trying to work out what has been going on and you held the key all the time.'

When Aunt Kit has gone Mumma gives Millie a hug. 'I'm really proud of you, Millie. You've been so clever. But this is dangerous work you've been doing. You did the right thing telling Ted and Joe.'

'I don't think it's fair. They've had all the fun. They left me out.'

Mumma takes Millie by the shoulders. 'Listen to me, Millie. What you did was very brave and very clever. But if Mr Albert or Mr Fisher had found out, you would have been in great danger. They would have thought nothing of hurting you to shut you up. It was right that you told Joe and Ted.'

159

'Joe and Annie are sweethearts.'

'And you instigated that too. Don't be sad at being left out, Millie. You've been there all along. Not in person, but in spirit.'

Millie thinks about this.

'I got Ted and Joe together.'

'And you gave Joe something worthwhile to do. He's a very different young man from the one you did your show to. And because he's feeling better, his leg's improving every day.'

'Martha thinks Ted should work at the hospital.'

'She's right. That's an excellent idea.'

'Will Papa be home soon?'

'I hope so Millie. I do hope so.'

Interlude 7

That evening Millie makes a decision. She'd been planning to visit Papa in France. She's pretty sure now that he's been tracking the same spy ring that she's helped to uncover. And she'd hoped she might see him on his way home. But from what Aunt Kit and Mumma have said, spying is dangerous work. What if she went to see him and found he'd been captured? There wouldn't be anything she could do to help. It would be terrible. And anyway she's still not sure that she hasn't dreamt it all along.

Before she gets into bed with Daisy, she takes the little acrobat from under her pillow. 'It's time to put you went back in the box,' she says. She opens the box lid, kisses the top of the little acrobat's head and whispers, 'Keep Papa safe.' Then she wraps him up in his ragged piece of tissue paper, pops him in the box, and closes the lid. When she looks up, Mumma is watching her and smiling.

Act 7

Mary has News

The long summer holidays are over and Millie and Mary have been back at school for a week. As usual Mary is waiting for Millie at the bottom of the steps, so they can walk to school together. She's always early, sitting there waiting as Millie comes down the last flight of steps. Today Millie can see she's itching to tell her something.

'Mam says the music hall has closed. There's rumours that it might open as a cinema soon, but not yet.'

'I know. Mumma told me that ages ago.'

'That's not fair. That was my news. Why didn't you tell me?'

Millie skips ahead. 'Oh, I don't know. Perhaps I thought you knew already.'

'Anyway,' Mary persists. 'Mam says it won't be long before Auntie Annie and Joe get engaged. She says they're right smitten.'

Millie laughs. Joe has stopped using his wheelchair now and is able to move quite quickly using his crutches.

'Does he mind going out with a canary?'

'I don't think so. They was in our front room canoodling last night and, I heard Joe tell Annie she was beautiful. Yuk.'

'Perhaps love makes you not notice some things,' Millie suggests.

'What things?'

'That she's got yellow skin.'

'She smells funny too. You can smell the factory on her.'

'Aunt Kit smells funny when she comes to see us. Even when she's in her pretty clothes, she smells like a bottle of Lysol. Her roses perfume can't cover it. It's 'cos she's always cleaning up, washing beds, and stuff. And she used to have white, smooth hands, but now they're red and sore.'

'She's still pretty, though.'

'Yes. And so is your Auntie Annie. And they're both strong, aren't they?'

'Yes, strong and pretty. Hope I'm like them when I grow up.'

'But not smelly.'

'No, not smelly.'

'Any news about yer Dad?' Millie shakes her head. 'He'll come 'ome. You'll see,' Mary calls as she runs to the school gate. Millie's not so sure.

An Announcement

When Miss Simpson reads the register that morning, she says she has a special announcement. 'I am delighted to tell you that Mrs Elliot is putting on a concert party for the poor men up at the hospital and in the convalescent home.' This is news to Millie.

'Mrs Elliot would like to invite a number of children to join her to entertain the wounded soldiers. Any questions?'

'What's a concert party, Miss?' Billie Fanshawe asks.

'It's like a show. Mrs Elliot thinks it might cheer them up. I think it's a very good idea.'

'Will we 'ave to see bad wounds, Miss?' Freda is looking concerned.

'No, you will be entertaining the men who are recovering. Many will be in the convalescent home. That's where they go when they're not ill enough for hospital, but not well enough for home. I need some children who would like to sing. And others who might like to dance.'

Lots of children put up their hands. Millie's keeps her hands on her desk. Mumma has said nothing about this to her. Left her out. She's blowed if she'll help. Why should she? Fancy not asking her. That's grown-ups for you.

Miss Simpson tells them that she's delighted that they are all so keen. 'I have a letter for your parents to tell them that we will need some rehearsal time after school.'

On the way home, Mary asks, 'Aren't you excited 'bout the show?' Millie shrugs. 'You didn't put your 'and up,' Mary persists. Millie shrugs again. She doesn't want to talk about it. Why hadn't Mumma told her?

'Got to go,' she says and runs off. She thinks about running away, going home, packing a bag and running away. If Mumma doesn't want her in the show, she'll never live it down. What will Ted say? People will laugh at her.

She runs up the stairs and bangs through the door. Mumma and Aunt Kit are sitting at table with teacups in front of them. 'Shsh,' they say together, putting a finger to their lips. Millie doesn't care if Daisy is asleep, she bangs her school bag down on the floor and shouts at Mumma, 'Why didn't you tell me about the concert party?'

'Shsh,' they say again and Aunt Kit gets up to guide her to the table.

'Millie, I forgot. I'm sorry.' Mumma's whispering.

'Well, I'm not going to be in the chorus line or a dancer.'

'Of course not,' says Mumma. 'The children are going to be singing and dancing to support you. You'll be singing just as you did for Joe and Grandad. Didn't Miss Simpson say?'

'Oh.' Millie is close to tears. She was so sure Mumma had left her out on purpose. Just then she hears a soft snore. Aunt Kit and Mumma look at each other and smile.

'Who's here?' Millie asks, and then sees that a man's army jacket is on the back of the chair. 'Is it Papa?' Millie gets up. Aunt Kit is at her side before she can look in Mumma's bed cupboard.

Mumma whispers, 'Just have a little look in at the door, and then you and I can go for a walk. If Kit doesn't mind staying to watch over Papa. That way we can talk more easily.'

Aunt Kit moves the cupboard door far enough for Millie to see. And there is Papa, fast asleep. He's not shaved and his skin's brown like it was when she saw him in *Brantôme*. He's snoring gently and is smiling. Is he really here? Millie puts her hand out to touch his shoulder very gently. Yes, he's real. At that moment he moves, and she snatches her hand back, scared she's woken him. But he resettles quickly. Millie just looks and looks. This is the best day of her whole life.

'Do you want a drink, Millie?' Aunt Kit whispers. 'You've only just got in from school.' Millie nods. Aunt Kit gets her a cup of milk and makes her a jam sandwich which she wraps in a napkin. Millie gulps the milk and then, clutching the sandwich, follows Mumma out.

Mumma Explains

Together Mumma and Millie walk towards the park. Millie has a tight hold of Mumma's hand.

'I'm sorry I forgot to tell you about the concerts, Millie. I had a telegram late last evening when you were fast asleep to tell me that Papa might be home today, but that nothing was certain. No time was given.'

'Why didn't you show me?'

'For no other reason than I didn't want to get your hopes up. If I'd shown you, and he hadn't come home, not only might you have been disappointed, but you might also have been frightened which is worse.'

They walk on. Millie thinks about what Mumma has said. It's true. What if she'd known and then Papa hadn't come home.

Mumma says, 'Getting a telegram can be a terrible thing. Do you remember when Martha was told that Joe had been injured?' Millie nods. 'But others have had worse news.'

'Can I see the telegram, please?'

'Let's sit down for a minute.'

They sit on the grass. The big wrought-iron benches with their green paint have long gone to the armaments factories to be made into weapons. Mumma takes a sheet of paper from her skirt pocket. It has thin strips of paper stuck to it which say –

PRIVATE FRANK ELLIOT LANDED IN ENGLAND 16TH SEPTEMBER 1915. EXPECT HOME ON LEAVE BY 19TH. UNCONFIRMED. REST PARAMOUNT.

'It was the *unconfirmed* that was so difficult. He had arrived back on the 16th as it says, but I didn't know that. He's been in a special debriefing session, reporting back. He's absolutely exhausted. His heart is troubling him. It always does when he gets over-tired. The army doctor saw him and said he could come home if he rested. Which is why I didn't want you to disturb him.'

'Is Daisy with Martha?' Mumma nods. 'Has she seen him?'

'No, Martha took her early and they were out looking for Grandad when Papa arrived. She hasn't seen him.'

Millie wants to ask what Papa has been doing. But she doubts Mumma would tell her. They'll be other ways of finding out. He's home, that's the main thing.

'Eat your sandwich, and then we must be getting back.' She gives Millie a hug. 'It's a good day, isn't it?'

Millie nods. It's the best day, but everything still feels uncertain. Unconfirmed, that was the word.

Papa

Papa slept for several hours after that. Martha had brought Daisy back all ready washed and in her nightdress, and they'd put her straight to bed. Millie knew there would be hell to pay if she told Daisy about Papa.

It had taken Millie ages to get to sleep that night. She'd lain awake going through her visits to France remembering *Bergerac*, *Brantôme*, the abbot, Marcel, Jacqueline, Eloise, the little Shetland pony, the caravan, the markets, and the golden coated llama.

When Mumma went to bed, she'd heard her say something very softly, and then everything was quiet again. By this time she was telling herself the story of *Treasure Island*, and as the pirate crew spotted land, Millie finally drifted asleep.

She wakes up to voices. Daisy's gone. She pushes back the door to her bed cupboard and sees Papa sitting at the table with Daisy on his knee. She's snuggled into him, still in her nightdress, and has her doll with her.

Catching sight of her, Papa says, 'You must have been as tired as I was, Millie. It's 9 o'clock.'

Oh no! Now she's late for school and she'll get a detention, do a hundred lines writing, *I must not be late for school*, over and over. And worse she'll have to leave Papa. She flops back on the bed. 'Why did you let me sleep in?' she says. And bursts into tears.

Papa is standing by her bed. 'Come on. Whatever are you crying about? Isn't this a happy day?'

'You're here and I've got to go to school, and now I'm late. And you're here, Papa, and I won't be.' She's sobbing now, trying to catch her breath.

Papa laughs. 'You're not going anywhere. We're going to spend the day together. Special dispensation. No school today.'

Mumma says, 'Come and have some breakfast, Millie. We've waited for you.'

'Get a move on, girl,' Papa says. 'I'm famished.'

Millie hops out of bed, dries her face on her nightdress and laughing, says, 'I need the toilet.' And then like a duchess, she says, 'Please do start without me!'

After breakfast, Papa had called on Martha and Joe, taking the girls with him. It had been fun. Martha had cried, of course, and given Papa a big hug and a kiss. But she'd told him off for being so thin. He'd laughed and told her life hadn't been the same without her nagging him. Papa and Joe had shaken hands and then given each other a hug. And said things like, 'Good work.'

'Not just me, Frank. Young Millie should be given the lion's share of the credit. It was her sharp eyes that spotted old Albert first.'

'Yes, I know,' Papa had said, ruffling Millie's hair. 'She's quite remarkable, this girl of mine.'

Papa and Joe had arranged to go out for a pint later.

'I'll check who's open today,' Joe had said. 'But we'll have to buy our own drinks, Frank. No standing rounds now there's a war on.'

Millie had explained, 'That's 'cos you mustn't owe anyone anything. Then they can't get you to do something you shouldn't.' They were all looking at her. Joe had his mouth open. 'We learnt that at school.'

'Things have changed in the short time I've been away,' Papa had said. 'Joe, your company will be my reward.'

'And yours mine, we've got lots to catch up on.'

'We have indeed,' Papa said.

Grandad had stood to attention and saluted Papa. Catching sight of Millie, he'd asked her to sing for him.

'Not just now, Grandad,' Papa had said. 'I'm going to be very selfish. My beautiful daughters are going to give all their time to me today.'

'Right you are, Sir,' Grandad had said. He'd stood to attention and saluted again.

Millie Gives Papa a Test

After lunch, Millie remembers the circus. 'We've got something to show you.' And Millie and Daisy bring out the two cardboard boxes and put them on the table. Papa is delighted.

'My goodness,' he says. 'Look at this. Let me see how you play with it.' So Millie assembles the three rings and then helps Daisy to unwrap the little figures.

'Look at this paper,' Papa says. 'To think it's the same I used to open when I played with the circus as a boy. Remarkable.'

Mumma has joined them. She picks up the little acrobat. 'This one is Millie's favourite,' she tells Papa. 'She used to wrap him in a hankie and he slept under her pillow whilst you were away.'

Millie is watching Papa. 'It's you, isn't it?' she tells him.

'Yes,' he says. And Millie senses that Papa is thinking about other places.

Deliberately, she picks up the white horse and the dancer. She's watching Papa intensely. 'This is Eloise, the beautiful white horse.' Papa looks at her, directly at her eyes. She can see something pass across his gaze, but she's not sure what.

'That's a good name. Very pretty.'

She picks up the dancer, but is still watching Papa. 'And this is Jacqueline,' she announces, pronouncing it in the French way.

This time there is the tiniest of reactions. 'Another pretty name.'

Millie says, 'And, do you know, she can do a very special trick. Whilst Eloise trots around the ring, Jacqueline can jump and turn in the air and then land on the horse's back.'

Mumma says, 'Goodness. There aren't many who can do that.'

Millie says, 'She can only do it when the horse is calm. It's too dangerous otherwise.'

'You know a lot about it, Millie,' Mumma says.

But Papa has turned his attention to Daisy and the animals she is tending. He's interested in the cardboard cage for the tiger. 'I had one of those, but it didn't survive very long. I'm pleased to see Samson has a new home.'

'He called Samthon,' Daisy says, lifting the tiger and kissing his nose. And they all laugh.

Another Test for Papa

A day or two later, Millie comes home from school and asks, 'Where's *Bergerac*?' Papa, who is reading the paper, mutters, 'Mmm?'

'Somewhere in France, isn't it?' Mumma says. 'Why do you want to know?'

'Oh, for a project at school,' Millie lies. She doesn't like to tell lies, but she needs to know if she's been dreaming or if she really did see Papa in France. And she can't ask him because it's all very secret. She's thought very hard about it. And now has a plan. Today she'll ask about *Bergerac*, but not *Brantôme*.

'Where's that old atlas you used to keep, Frank?' Mumma asks. 'We might find it there.'

He doesn't want to look. Millie can see that. Normally he'd be up immediately and find the atlas, keen to help her with her work for school.

'Come on, Frank,' Mumma says. 'Help the child.'

He gets up reluctantly and goes to the cupboard, takes out the large atlas and puts it on the table. 'Why *Bergerac*?' he asks.

Millie's ready with her answer, 'Oh, we're looking at French towns which start with the letter B.'

'I see.' He opens the huge book and looks at the contents page for France. Then opens the book at pages 13 and 14.

'I still don't understand why you have thought of *Bergerac*. Why not *Boulogne* or *Bordeaux*? They are much more important to France.'

'I like the name,' Millie says. '*Bergerac*. I chose it because it sounded nice.'

Mumma is really interested in the map and asks Papa if he has heard of *Bergerac* before.

He tells her that it's a place that makes nice wine, not as grand as *Burgundy*, but pleasant none the less.

'Have you drunk some then?' Mumma has taken over the questioning, in a gentle, interested way, but Millie is listening intently to Papa's answers. He's not looking at them at all, just concentrating on the map.

'Yes, I have drunk *Bergerac Rouge*, and it's a light wine, very nice.'

'Come on, then. Where in France, is it? Don't they have a list of place names at the back of this great tome?'

'We could look at the index,' Papa says. Millie can see Mumma's beaten his resistance. 'But even then it might not be in here. It isn't a major town. But let's look.'

Papa moves a finger slowly over the page as if he's pretending to look for the town. But Millie can see that he knows where it is.

'Yes, here it is. *Bergerac*. East of *Bordeaux* in the *Dordogne* region.'

'Are people fighting in that part of France?' Mumma asks.

'No, the war is being waged much further north. This is a long way away from the fighting.'

'What's the town like?' Millie asks.

Papa looks exasperated. 'How am I expected to know that, Millie?'

'That's enough geography for one day,' Mumma says. 'Frank, you look very tired, my dear. Why not put your feet up and rest? You're out with Joe tonight and you want to be on good form.'

Papa seems relieved and gives Mumma a kiss. He heads for their bed cupboard, takes off his boots and disappears behind the door.

Millie knows now that *Bergerac* does exist, and she is determined to find out more.

Rehearsals

Millie wants to check out what she's seen in France, but every bit of spare time over the next few days is used up on the rehearsals for the concert party.

There are two parts to the concert. The first where Millie and the children perform, and the second where Mumma performs. Mumma was hoping that some of her friends from the music hall would be able to join her, but many are away touring, performing in other cities. Why wouldn't they want to help the wounded soldiers?

'They're not as lucky as we are,' Mumma had explained. 'They have to keep working or they won't eat.'

If Papa is around for any of the concerts, he'll play the piano - a solo piece, ragtime, he thinks. Millie hopes he'll be there.

Miss Simpson has allowed them to practise in the school hall and has offered to accompany the performance on the piano.

Millie's bit is easy. She knows all the songs and how to perform them. The problem is getting the children to remember their words and moves.

Archie Fanshawe always follows his twin brother, Billie. But Billie often gets it wrong and everyone ends up in a muddle. It reminds Millie of the new recruits in the park. She tries hard not to laugh. But Mumma is very patient and eventually, they have learned the choruses of all the songs, and the marching and dance moves.

One evening as they are clearing away the supper dishes, Mumma says, 'During the concert, you must take responsibility for what is happening behind you, Millie.'

'Why? I've got enough to do remembering my own moves and the words and the tune.'

'Well, if you want to be a real star, and not just a pretend one, you'll have to learn to help your support act. It's not just about you. When you're not singing you should step to the side to let the audience see the others on stage, and give the other children a clap when they've finished. You're part of a team out there.'

Millie's not so sure. That wasn't in her plan.

Mumma gives her hug. 'You can do it, Millie, because I've seen you do it with Daisy when she's been dancing.'

Treasure

One evening after rehearsals, Aunt Kit comes for supper and to see how Papa is.

'My, you look more rested,' she tells him.

'Yes, it's good to be back with my lovely girls.'

'Have you seen the toy circus? You didn't mind my giving it to the girls?'

'No. They've looked after it perfectly. So no. It's fine.'

Millie looks at Papa. He doesn't sound too sure. 'We do look after it, Papa,' she tells him.

'I know you do. And toys need to be played with, of course they do.'

'I've got something else for Millie,' Aunt Kit says. And she digs deep into her bag. She brings out a long cardboard box with the words *Hogarth and Hayes Drawing Pencils* on the lid. 'These are so small that I've had to get a new set, but Millie might be able to get some use out of them. Her fingers are smaller than mine.'

As she opens the box, Millie gasps. Normally she has to write on a slate with chalk, or use a simple grey lead pencil on bits of paper. In the box are the short stubs of about 12 coloured pencils. They can't be more than 2 inches long. Each has a sharp point, sharpened with a knife.

Aunt Kit says, 'They're far too short for me. I can't control them. But it seemed a shame to waste them.'

Millie picks out the colours and puts them on the table, blue, red, yellow, brown, green. They are like treasure. She jumps up and hugs Aunt Kit. 'Thank you. Thank you.'

'Thank you, Kit,' Papa says.

'And I thought you'd like your own drawing book. Will you take care of it, Millie? Don't waste it. I'd like to see what you've drawn, next time I come.'

Millie looks at the book. It is about the size of *Treasure Island*, but is much thinner. It has a thin brown paper cover, but inside she counts six sheets of plain paper fixed together by two staples in the middle of the book. 'That means I've got space for twenty-four pictures.'

'Well, let's hope the pencil stubs last long enough to allow you to do all that drawing,' Aunt Kit says laughing. 'Of course, you could always do some writing with a lead pencil to fill up some of the spaces.'

As the grown-ups talk, Millie starts work on the book. She puts her name on the front using all the different colours.

MILLIE ELLIOT Aged 9

Then she turns to the centre of the book so that she has a double page in front of her and begins to draw. At one point, Papa says he's going for some fish and chips for supper.

'I'll come,' says Aunt Kit. 'What about you, Millie?'

'No, I'm going to stay with Mumma and do my drawing, thank you.'

'Oh, well, we'll take Daisy then. Come along Daise, get your coat.'

Millie has to stop drawing when they return with the hot steamy pieces of fish in their golden batter. She steals a chip from a plate, getting a slap on the back of her hand in return. The chip is worth it, still hot, and crunchy and soft at the same time.

'Did you bring any batter bits?' Millie asks.

'Of course, and mushy peas.'

'And you won't be getting anything, unless you sit down and eat this like a lady, instead of a gutter snipe,' Mumma says, suddenly losing patience.

Aunt Kit is shocked. 'Millie, please sit down and do as you are told.'

Millie isn't worried. Mumma's worried about Papa. That's all and the slap didn't hurt. She gets water for Daisy and herself and glasses for the beer Papa has brought for Mumma, Kit and himself.

'This is the food of the gods,' says Papa. 'These are very good, but the very best are when you sit on a sea wall, looking out across to the horizon as the sun is setting, eating fish and chips with lashings of vinegar, out of newspaper.' And then more grandly, he says, 'It's the print, you know, that augments the taste.'

They all laugh, the tension has gone. He's done it again!

Another Test for Papa

By the time, Aunt Kit is ready to go back to the hospital, Millie's finished her picture. She's drawn the circus tent with the red sides and the blue roof with the yellow star. Alongside it she's drawn the cream and red gypsy caravan with its big wheels, and steps, and a stable door with the top half open. She has a sign too which says, *Circus Suisse.*

'Millie,' Mumma says. 'That's remarkable.'

'My pencil stubs are in safe hands. What a clever girl, you are.'

Millie and Daisy go to the door to wave Aunt Kit good-bye. It's been such a happy evening. When she turns back into the room though, she is terrified by what she sees. Papa is standing in front of the picture and he looks like he's seen a ghost. His sunburned skin has drained of all colour. And he's holding his chest, trying to breathe. She's reminded of Ted and his asthma.

Mumma rushes over to him. 'Frank, my dear. You've overtired yourself again. Come, my dear, sit by the fire and I'll get you some brandy.'

Daisy has started to cry. Mumma says, 'Millie, get yourself and Daisy ready for bed.' And before Millie can protest or ask her about Papa, Mumma says, 'Now. This minute.'

Millie collects up the pencil stubs, puts them back in the box. She closes, her book, but as she walks to put them in the cupboard, Papa puts out his hand.

'May I see your picture again, please?' Millie's not sure. He looked like he hated her drawing.

As if reading her mind, Papa says, 'I won't damage your book, Millie. I'd like to look at it. It's such a good job you've done.'

When she and Daisy are ready for bed, they come over to give him a kiss good-night. Papa closes the book, gives it to Millie and says, 'You'll need to keep that safe. It's an excellent picture, but please don't show it to anyone else. Will you promise me, Millie?' Millie nods. 'Good girl. Now off to bed, and let your poor old Papa rest.'

Papa and Millie Share Secrets

Millie and Mary had been planning to go to the park to do some final rehearsing for the concert. But as they reach the gate, Millie sees Papa waiting. He's still looking as serious as he has over the past few days. It's as if he hasn't been with them.

Papa says to Mary, 'Do you mind if I steal Millie from you, Mary? There's something that we have to do, my dear.'

'See you tomorrow,' Mary calls as she runs off.

'Where are we going?' Millie asks.

'You'll see.'

Papa and Millie head into town and Millie realises that they're going to the theatre. It's all shut up now. Has been since Mr Albert was arrested. People had said the show hadn't been the same once Mumma had retired. Anyway there were other theatres they could go to.

Papa leads her, along the alley at the side of the theatre, to the Stage Door. He takes a large bunch of keys from his pocket and opens the door. 'I'll go first,' he says.

At the side of the door is a large switch that turns on the backstage lights. There's a loud buzz, and then a dim glow which gets ever brighter. As the switch clunks, Millie hears the scamper of little feet. She hopes its only mice. Papa closes the door behind them.

He leads her past Mumma's dressing room with its green door and silver stars. Then past the chorus girls' dressing room. Everywhere smells dusty. There's old sweat in the air, and she can smell the moth balls from the costumes, and a hint of oily greasepaint. And Lysol as they come near the toilet. She sees how old and battered everything looks without the people.

They walk past Mr Albert's office where she'd found the notebook and heard the argument, and up onto the stage. The huge red curtains are closed, so she can't see the auditorium with its rows of seats and ashtray boxes. It's cold in here. Millie shivers. She hadn't expected to.

Here, too, is the large props basket where she used to sit, and where Aunt Kit had joined her that evening when she'd heard Mr Fisher say he wanted Mr Albert to take out a canary.

Papa is speaking again. 'This is your spot, isn't it, Millie? Your perch?' Millie nods. 'Shall we sit here?' he asks. They both sit on the basket and Millie realises that her feet can now touch the floor. She must have grown over the summer.

'Why are we here, Papa?'

'We have something to sort out, you and I, and I wanted somewhere where we could be private and not overheard.' Millie waits. 'I think you have some explaining to do, young lady.'

Millie has learned that it's better to let grown-ups tell you what they think you've done wrong. If you try and guess, you get into even more trouble. Don't own up to anything, until you know for certain.

'I'm really thirsty,' Millie says. 'And hungry. Mumma always has something ready after school to eat and drink. Should we go home?'

Papa takes a small bottle of lemonade out of one pocket and an apple out of another. The stopper of the bottle is held with a metal clamp. As Papa unclips this, the lemonade hisses at them. Millie's mouth waters. Lemonade is a treat. He wipes the apple on his sleeve, and hands both to Millie.

'All right,' Papa says. 'Let's start with the French project, shall we?' Millie is looking at her apple and lemonade. 'There is no French project, is there?' Millie shakes her head.

'So now, what was all that stuff about French towns beginning with B? And, *Bergerac*, in particular?'

'I had a dream that you were in France and in *Bergerac*. And I wondered where it was.'

'Well, now you know, it's in the *Dordogne* region, towards the south-west of the country.'

Millie just nods.

'Go on. There's something else to this B town question. What is it?'

Millie looks up at Papa and his face is gentle, but she can see his concern.

'I need to know all about this, Millie. It is vital to the war effort. I need to know how you know about *Bergerac*. Did you hear it from Mr Albert?'

Millie is shocked. 'Oh no, Papa.'

'Then how?'

'The little acrobat.' She's been dreading telling him the truth.

She's sure he won't believe her. He'll think she's mad, have her locked away from the family.

'This little fellow?' Papa asks, taking the little figure from his pocket. Millie nods.

'Right, young lady. I want it all, from the very beginning.'

So, sitting there on the props basket, Millie tells Papa all about the little acrobat and how when she kissed the top of his head and said *Take my love to Papa, Acrobat* she was taken away, from her home and her bed, to France.

She tells of seeing him first on the quayside. How she saw him settle the horse, Chester, and how she'd seen Joe march down the gangplank. How she'd heard the conversation with the Captain on the ship and how she'd seen Papa head off in a cart.

'When did this visiting occur?'

'Usually, it was only at night and when I was alone, that I could see you. When Daisy was in with Mumma.'

'How often did you visit?'

'No more than four times. The first was the ship, the second *Bergerac*, the third was at the circus when you pasted up the circus posters in *Brantôme*, and the last time was when you went to see the man near the bridge in *Brantôme* and Jacqueline did the somersault on Eloise.'

'Did you see me at any other time?'

'No. Later, I realised that what you were doing was really dangerous, but that you were on your way home. I don't know what I would have done if I was there and you were captured or something. So I didn't go again. Just told the little acrobat to keep you safe.'

'Tell me about *Bergerac.*'

So Millie tells him all about the market and Marcel and how she thought Papa didn't trust him.

'Quite right,' he says. 'Very observant.'

'I saw the Shetland Pony, Paulette, and Eloise, and Spitz, the golden llama. They had a funny stable out in the market place. And it was warm and the hot pebbles burned my feet, but not really. They weren't sore in the morning.'

Papa laughed at that. 'That's good,' he said. 'Have you told anyone about these things that you saw?'

'No, Papa. That wouldn't have been safe. I haven't told anyone at all. I promise you.'

'I'm impressed, Millie, that you can be so young and yet so discrete.'

Millie is in the middle of telling him about the cart trip to *Brantôme*, when she suddenly realises something. 'You aren't surprised, are you?'

'What do you mean?' It's his turn to be careful now.

'You aren't surprised that I could see you with the help of the little acrobat. You believe me, don't you? You know!'

'Carry on with your story, and then I'll tell you. It's important you tell me everything first.'

So Millie returns to the trip to *Brantôme*. Even she's surprised at how much she can remember. She tells Papa about the children, and the Abbot and the monks walking in the caves behind the church. 'When I went again, you had written us a letter, and you had to burn it up and throw it in the river. When I saw the letter, I knew you still loved us. That you weren't going to forget us and stay with Jacqueline.'

'No, Jacqueline meant nothing to me. But unfortunately you have to use people so that the right things can be done.'

'Like Auntie Annie said she would pretend to Mr Albert that she liked him and that she'd tell him the name of the acrobat grenade.'

'Yes, just like that. Did she tell you the name of the grenade?'

'Oh no. Joe asked her, but she wouldn't tell him. And anyway if a thing's a secret, it mustn't be told. It was the man by the bridge, who said. That was the final piece, wasn't it? It was acrobat grenades,'

Papa nods. 'We needed something that was a name that could be recognised, thought to be real, but which couldn't be muddled with anything that was really being manufactured in the armaments factories anywhere in Great Britain.'

'So when you heard it in France, you knew someone was spying and passing information on.'

'Yes. And with the connections that you, Joe, Ted and Annie made, we knew who that was. We were able to close the loop.'

Papa looks around. 'This is a fine old place,' he says. 'Sad that it won't be used for shows anymore.'

'Why not?'

'Because there are too many theatres already, and we need places to show the new moving pictures.'

'We could do the concert parties here,' Millie says.

'No. The concert parties must be done where the men are. It's easier for those of us who can walk to go to perform for them where they are being cared for. It would be too difficult to fill the theatre with wounded soldiers. Anyway, this is earmarked as a cinema.'

'Are you going back to be a spy again?'

'Not for a while. But I won't be at home, of course. I'm still in the army and it has plenty of work for me to do. But mainly in England.'

Papa asks Millie to finish telling him about her trips to France. When she's done, she asks Papa what's happened to the circus.

'Oh, it's still travelling around France.'

'Will it ever come to England?'

'No, it would be too expensive to bring all the animals across the Channel.'

Millie's pleased about that. Having the circus here would complicate things.

'Look at me, Millie. I need you to know something very important.' She looks at him. Papa is very serious. 'You need to realise that you must never refer to what you have seen ever again. Do you understand?' Millie nods. 'No, that's not enough, Millie. I need you to say it.'

'I promise, Papa.'

'That's not enough, say what you promise.'

'I promise not to tell anyone anything about what I've seen.'

'Good. But you must realise that you have already told people because you have mentioned *Bergerac*. And worse you have drawn and named the circus.' Millie is shocked. She hadn't thought. She just needed to know, to be sure. Thought she was being clever. But she'd told Mumma about *Bergerac* and she'd written the words *Circus Suisse.*

'I don't want you to change your picture, Millie. But perhaps you could change the name of the circus. Let's think about that on the way home.'

Papa starts to get up. 'Come on. We'd better be getting back to your mother.'

Millie doesn't move. 'You haven't told me how you know I've been telling you the truth. How you know about the little acrobat.'

'Oh, that's simple. Because he transported me too. Although, everyone thought I was happy at my boarding school, I wasn't. I missed my family, my parents, my brother and sister. I was very lonely. I had taken the little acrobat from the toy circus and kept him safe away from the other boys. When I was feeling very alone, I would take him out, kiss his head and say very quietly, *I wish I was away from here.* And for a few hours, I was taken away. To the world of the circus.'

'Is that why you ran away?'

'Yes. The little acrobat showed me another world. Oh, I saw that it wasn't an easy world. That you had to work hard. And that you lived in very cramped conditions, but those visits were such fun. And it soon was not enough to just visit, I wanted to be a real part of it. So I ran away.'

'Golly.'

'Golly, indeed. But I promised Mumma we'd be back in time for supper and we mustn't be late.'

At the Stage-Door once more, he says, 'This has to be our secret, Millie. You know that don't you? Say it.'

'Yes, Papa.'

'Good girl.' And he turns off the light switch with a clunk and the passageway returns to darkness. When they are out in the sunshine again, he shuts the door with a loud clang and they head off home.

Dress Rehearsal

Everyone is very excited because the concert party is due to take place in two days' time. The children are almost word perfect and, now that Millie is encouraging them, they are more confident with the moves.

Martha has been busy too. Mumma's given her some old pantomime costumes from the theatre and she's altered them for the children. They'll look like gypsy boys and girls. Millie likes her silky red skirt and white cotton blouse with puffy sleeves. But most of all, she likes the little dark blue velvet bolero with strings that hold the edges together, like a shoe lace. Mary agrees. She likes wearing hers too. The boys have black trousers and white blousy shirts with green felt waistcoats.

It's the last time they'll practice together and they all wear their costumes and go through their whole performance, from start to finish. Some things go wrong, like Freda tripping over, and even Millie missed a verse of Daisy Belle, but Mumma says that if something doesn't go wrong during the dress rehearsal, the main show might be a disaster.

A man comes along to take their photograph. He takes ages setting up. He fixes the heavy camera onto a wooden stand which has three long legs. When they're all assembled in a group, and after lots of pushing and shoving from the boys, the man covers the camera and himself with a big black cloth and holds a light high in the air above his head. He shouts, 'Say Cheese, please.' And as they all shout 'Cheese, please' and laugh, he presses a button. There's an almighty pop and flash, like the light has blown up, and the photograph is taken.

For a little while afterwards, they can only see spots in front of their eyes, but Billy Fanshawe says he's got worms. Mumma lets out an enormous laugh. And Miss Simpson tells Billy that she thinks he means he can see worms in his eyes. 'That's right,' he says. 'Worms in me eyes.'

'Good luck, everyone,' Miss Simpson says. 'I'm sure you'll be excellent and really cheer up our brave heroes.'

The Show

And, at last, today is the day of the show.

The children have been told that they must meet at the front of the convalescent home after lunch. It's a big old building with wide stone steps going up to a double door. A porter and Aunt Kit are there to meet them. Aunt Kit introduces Miss Simpson and Mumma to the porter. His name is Mr Jones.

'Just call me Jones,' he tells them. 'Everyone else does.'

Aunt Kit says, 'Thank you so much for coming. I must go back to help the patients get ready for the concert. But Jones will look after you and show you where to go. See you soon.'

Jones leads them down a long corridor. On one side there are big windows and on the other side are doors. The floor is made from black and white tiles and their feet clatter as they walk over it.

When they get near the end of the corridor, a tall lady with white hair and a dark blue dress comes to meet them. She has no apron, but she wears a dark blue belt with a silver buckle. Millie can see she's a nurse. On top of her head, over her white curly hair, she wears a white hat which has frilly lace around the top. She says, 'Ah, I heard you coming. These floors are so unforgiving. Good afternoon.'

She shows them into a large room. The ceiling is so high that they have to bend backwards to see the pretty, knobbly pattern along the top of the walls and around the great lights which hang from the ceiling. These remind Millie of the chandelier at the theatre. Near the door is a large low platform which will be their stage. There's a piano near the wall at the other side. There are lines of chairs at the back of the room, but a large open area at the front.

'Why will everyone be sitting so far away from us?' Mary asks Miss Simpson.

'They won't. The space at the front is for the men who need to use wheel chairs.'

Jones says, 'Matron, if you don't need me anymore, I'll go and help on the wards.'

'Thank you, Jones.' And then to them, she says, 'Thank you so much for coming. When VAD Elliot told me of the idea of a concert party, I thought it was remarkable. The men are really looking forward to it.'

Matron shows them into a smaller room behind the big room, and says that this is where they can change into their costumes. 'I understand your husband is coming today, Mrs Elliot. And Major Palmer from the Ministry of Information. We are honoured.'

'Frank wanted to be able to play at the first concert. I'm very pleased he can join us,' Mumma says.

'And we have some other visitors too, I believe.'

'Yes, Martha's son, Joe, and her father-in-law are coming too. Martha made our costumes for us. And Mary's, Auntie Annie. And they'll be bringing little Daisy, Millie's younger sister.'

'Well, they're all very welcome. But I expect you'd really like to get ready. The audience will be arriving very shortly.' She leaves them.

'Get into your costumes, please,' says Miss Simpson. There's lots of excitement as they take off their everyday clothes and line up to receive the costumes. 'Let's keep the room tidy,' Miss Simpson says. 'We'll need to change again quickly at the end of the performance.'

When Millie walks out onto the stage with her friends, she cannot believe her eyes. In front of them are lots of men in blue uniforms. Some are sitting on ordinary chairs towards the back of the room. Others are in wheelchairs, and one or two are in bath chairs. There are nurses sitting around the room too and porters, and she can see Ted in his new porter's uniform.

Everyone cheers when they see the children.

Looking into the room, Millie sees Aunt Kit with a patient in one of the bath chairs. They share a smile. She sees Joe, Auntie Annie, Grandad, Martha and a waving Daisy. Papa is there too with a man. Both are in army uniform. He must be Major Palmer.

Looking at the patients, Millie wonders if they'd been at the station when she went to meet Papa with Mumma. She'd been worried that the soldiers would still have lots of bandages, but only a few have bandages and those are clean. None have the scarlet splashes she'd seen before. She's feeling very nervous and quite sick now. She's sure she's forgotten the words of the songs. She can't even remember which song comes first. She starts to shake.

Miss Simpson sits at the piano and plays the opening bars of *It's a Long Way to Tipperary*, Millie hears the marching feet of her friends behind her, and everything comes flooding back. As she starts to march on the spot, and she sings the opening verse, the audience gives an almighty cheer. When she gets to the chorus, everyone is joining in.

Then they sing *Pack Up Your Troubles in Your Old Kit Bag*. It's a new song, but it's very popular because it says people should smile through their troubles. Millie tries to remember to smile as she sings and the poor wounded soldiers smile back at her.

There's another huge cheer as the Fanshawe twins get their moves muddled. They both step forward and bow, before rushing back to find their places which pleases the audience.

Their last song is *Daisy Belle*. As they sing the last line, there are whistles and cheers and shouts of 'Bravo', just like Millie has heard at the music hall when Mumma has been singing. And Papa and Major Palmer are cheering too. And Miss Simpson is standing by the piano clapping with her hands up in the air.

When they all come forward to take their bow, Mary whispers. 'Weren't we good?'

Millie says, 'You were brilliant.'

The children are told to sit on the floor in front of the stage. And just as they do at school, they sit cross-legged in a row.

Matron comes up to the stage and says, 'What a truly wonderful melody of songs from such a talented group of young people. Thank you so much. We are ready to go on, I think, but should we have a short break?' Someone must have answered her, because she then says, 'No? Well, let the show continue.'

Papa comes forward to play the piano. Before he starts, he has to wave at Daisy who is calling to him. He bows to the audience, and flexes his fingers.

'I thought a Beethoven Sonata might be appropriate,' he tells the audience, using a very posh voice. 'Or maybe some

Rachmaninov.'

'Bring on the kids again,' someone shouts. And others seem to agree. Oh dear. What if they don't like him?

'But,' Papa says loudly. 'Knowing what an artistic, inventive, egalitarian lot you are, we have something a little more cultural.' A real cheer goes up. He's teasing them and they know it. She's heard it before at the theatre. At the piano, Papa plays *The Maple Leaf Rag* and then *The Entertainer.* He's so clever, his fingers are very fast on the keys, and the music twinkles in the air. The audience joins in when they can by clapping in time to the music. It's difficult with the first piece, much easier the second.

At the end, Papa stands and gives a very low bow. And as he walks back to join Major Palmer, the soldiers closest to him, reach out and shake his hand.

And now it's Mumma's turn. Miss Simpson once more goes to the piano. Mumma's songs are much slower than the children's, less marching. But all of them are popular. Her voice, too, is gentler than when she's singing in the theatre.

The first one is one Millie knows soldiers sing often themselves. It's called *Keep the Home Fires Burning,*

Whilst she sings *There's a Long, Long Trail A-Winding,* The men in the audience hum the tune.

The audience cheers as she starts to sing the next song *After the Ball* and Mumma pretends to dance just like she might at a real ball

She finishes with *Let Me Call You Sweetheart.* It's the song she sang to Grandad. Millie looks back at the audience. The men are concentrating on Mumma and some are swaying in their seats in time to the music.

The cheering at the end is so loud Millie has to put her hands over her ears. Mumma goes over and brings Miss Simpson up on the stage and they take a bow together, then she calls Papa, and finally all the children. They take four curtain calls. Going out through the big door, waiting a few minutes and then running back on stage to more cheers and whistles.

Matron puts an end to it. She stands on the stage and puts her hands up. No-one argues with her. The men who had been standing, sit down. The noisy ones stop whistling and cheering.

'My goodness,' she says. 'What a wonderful afternoon. And we aren't finished yet. We have one unscheduled part of the proceedings. Are we safe to continue?'

All agree, so she suggests that those on stage return to their seats and invites Major Palmer to join her.

A Surprise

Major Palmer marches up on stage. He hands a cardboard box to Matron. There is an air of expectation in the room, people are whispering.

'Matron, ladies and gentlemen, servicemen, nurses, children. It gives me great pleasure to bestow some awards on some very special people gathered in this room. This is not about valour on the battlefield. It is about common sense and a deep sense of duty on the home front. This group of people have helped to crush a dangerous ring of spies selling information to the enemy. As you will understand I am unable to go into detail about their activity, suffice it to say they have helped the war effort considerably.

First of all, please give a warm welcome to Miss Ann Townsend who is not only involved in the manufacture of the weapons we all need, but who engaged one of the agents directly.'

Auntie Annie walks forward and onto the stage. She's smiling. There's loud cheering and whistling. Major Palmer takes something from Matron and pins it to Auntie Annie's collar. It's a gold medal. 'Well done, he says. 'And thank you, Miss Townsend.'

Major Palmer gives Auntie Annie time to get back to her place and then says, 'Joe Harris.'

Joe comes forward. He's wearing his blue uniform, but walking now with a stick. He receives a Certificate of Commendation. 'Well done, Private. Great work,' Major Palmer tells him. More cheering. Millie claps and claps. She looks around at Martha who is dabbing a hankie to her face, but looks so happy. Grandad salutes Joe as he returns, and Joe salutes him back.

'For helping the effort and ensuring mobility, Ted Jarvis.' More cheering. Ted receives a Certificate of Commendation too. 'Congratulations, young man,' Major Palmer says.

Major Palmer then looks out over the audience. 'This whole operation on the home front was initiated because one young lady watched, noticed things, made connections. She is the youngest person ever to receive such an award. We should all follow her example. Miss Millie Elliot.'

She can't believe it. Major Palmer has called her to the stage. The noise in the room is astonishing. She can feel the floor bounce as the men stamp their feet, clap and whistle. Mary gives her a nudge. 'Go on. Get up there.'

Mumma comes down and takes her hand. Millie is a little alarmed that Major Palmer might stick the pin in her, and perhaps sensing her nervousness, he suggests that Matron might give Millie her award. But someone else takes the gold medal from Matron. And it is Papa who pins the medal to Millie's bolero.

'You deserve this, Millie.' he says. 'Well done.'

Major Palmer shakes her hand. 'You've been very brave. Just like your Papa. Well done, my dear.'

Everyone claps and Mumma asks all the children and Miss Simpson to come on stage and with Papa at the piano, everyone sings *God Save the King*. Millie thinks she might burst with pride.

At Home

In bed that night, Millie looks back on the afternoon. Matron had invited them to share tea with the patients. There'd been sandwiches and cakes, and lemonade for the children and tea for the adults.

People had asked to see her medal. And had asked her about what she'd done to catch the spies. She'd told them only that she'd noticed a man writing things about them as they joined up. And Joe said, 'We always said they knew we was coming, didn't we?' And they'd become very serious and nodded their heads.

Matron has asked that they might come back again. Perhaps not in such a grand way, but to give smaller concerts each fortnight for the individual wards. Matron had suggested that Mumma and Aunt Kit should organise it.

She remembers how grand the home had been. Not really like a hospital. Johnny Handley had asked if the frames around the pictures hanging on the wall were real gold. People had laughed, but that wasn't fair because she'd wondered about that too.

Finale

Papa has gone again now. But he's working in England with the army. Mumma says he can't tell them what he's doing. And Millie understands. But that doesn't stop her missing him.

She's almost finished her drawing book. She looks back at the first picture she'd drawn. She feels like she's back at the circus with Papa. She can remember the warm days on her visits to France. She'd promised Papa that she wouldn't do or say anything else that would let people know what he'd been doing in France. And she'd kept her promise. All the other pictures she'd drawn were of her friends and places near her home. And some of the toy circus figures too. So the little acrobat is there, and the tiger, and the ringmaster. And the white horse and the dancer are there too, but they have new names. The horse is now called Misty and the dancer is Marie. Papa hadn't told her to change them. But you can't be too careful. There's a picture of the big tree in the park and her school. And the theatre with the trapeze artists, The Carlton Brothers.

'There,' she says. 'I've finished.'

'Let me see,' Mumma says. Millie shows her.

'I think one of the best pictures is the first one you did, Millie. The circus.'

'Yes. It's the one I like best too. And the little acrobat.'

'You know, I could have sworn you've changed the name of the circus. It wasn't *Circus Saissa* originally, was it?'

'Yes, but I'd spelt it wrong and Papa helped me to get the right spelling. It's a real place. I saw it in Papa's atlas.'

Daisy asks Millie to play with the circus with her. Millie's pleased to be able to close the book and not to have to answer any more difficult questions.

She takes the three wooden circles and fits them together in their familiar clover leaf shape. Daisy is already releasing the tiger and the other figures.

'No, little acrobat,' Daisy says, and she starts to dig amongst the tissue paper. It is getting very torn now.

'No, he isn't here anymore,' Millie said. 'But don't worry, he'll be back.'

Author's Note

My sister, Judy, and I grew up with the stories our mother, Mollie, told us about her parents and her life as a little girl growing up during World War 1. The war was the backdrop to her earliest years and she remembered – new soldiers training in the park, the injured soldiers returning from the battlefront, the ladies who were nurses helps (Voluntary Aid Detachments – VADs - just like Aunt Kit), and the women who gave white feathers to men who did not have a uniform.

There were memories too about the music hall. The large wicker props basket was Mollie's seat in the big theatres the family travelled to, and we were told of the noise and bustle as she watched her mother singing on the stage.

As a young man, our grandfather, Samuel Copeman, did run away to join a circus and to work with horses. Later he became an acrobat, tightrope walker and trapeze artiste. But unlike Frank Elliot in the story, Samuel came from a poor family. He ran away from home so he didn't have to work in the boot factory in Norwich.

Our grandmother came from a music hall family. She was a singer, dancer and pianist and her stage name was Dolly Caffrey. She performed in pantomimes and shows, and Mollie remembered travelling with her to summer season in Morecombe. Dolly may not have been a star on stage, but those who knew her thought she was a kind and very special lady.

Although the story is inspired by family memories, the characters in the book are not Florence, Sam or Mollie. Both Florence and Mollie were strong women and I hope that comes across in the story. And I wrote the story because I wanted a way of showing what life might have been like 100 years ago for a little girl.

My grand-daughter, Isobelle Greaves has provided the lovely illustrations for the book and I am delighted she could help me with this project.

The songs that Florence, Millie and her friends sing were all very popular at the time. You can find them on YouTube, sometimes with very old recordings.

Your King and Country Want You by *Paul Rubens* (1914)

Daisy Belle by *Harry Dacre (1892)*

Pop Goes the Weasel is an old nursery song first published around *1850*

It's a Long Way to Tipperary by *Jack Judge (1912)*

Molly Malone is an old Irish song about a seller of seafood from the 19th century.

Let Me Call You Sweetheart by Friedman and Whitson (1910)

Pack Up Your Troubles by *George and Felix Powell (George Asaf) (1915)*

The Maple Leaf Rag by *Scott Joplin (1899)*

The Entertainer by *Scott Joplin (1902)*

Keep the Home Fires Burning by *Ivor Novello and Lena G Ford (1914)*

There's a Long, Long Trail A-Winding by *Stoddart King and Alonzo*

Elliot (1914)

After the Ball is Over by *Charles K Harris (1891)*

And the circus? When Judy and I went to visit our own Aunt Kit we would be sent to the front parlour of her little house in Saffron Walden and allowed to play with the old toy circus, with its trefoil rings, lead figures, and I am sure there was a little acrobat waiting patiently for his next adventure…………..

ABOUT THE AUTHOR

Kate Greaves is a writer of prose and poetry. In 2015, she achieved an MA in Creative Writing with the University of Southampton. She lives in Hampshire with her husband, Mike, an artist and illustrator. They have two children and four grand-children.

Printed in Great Britain
by Amazon